Readers love the Faith, series by TERE

### *Faith & Fidelity*

"I cried… before the prologue was even finished. I mean the story hadn't even started and I was a mess! I just do not seem to have the words to say how much I enjoyed this emotional roller coaster."

—Prism Book Alliance

"A lovely, poignant story with heart. I recommend this to any m/m reader, especially if you're just venturing into the genre."

—Sinfully Sexy Book Reviews

### *Love & Loyalty*

"Be prepared to laugh a bunch, shed a few tears, and jump for joy when these two find their happy ever after."

—Love Bytes

"This was an amazing addition to Tere Michaels' Faith, Love, and Devotion series. I look forward to reading many more books by this author. Highly recommended."

—The Novel Approach

### *Duty & Devotion*

"Those familiar with this author are aware of her talents and her strengths for writing multi-dimensional characters, intelligent dialogue and believable story lines… she has quickly become a favourite author among many readers within the sub-genre."

—The Indie Reviewer

By TERE MICHAELS

One Holiday Ever After (Multiple Author Anthology)
One Night Ever After (Multiple Author Anthology)
Who Knows the Storm

FAITH, LOVE, AND DEVOTION
Faith & Fidelity
Love & Loyalty
Duty & Devotion
Cherish & Blessed
Truth & Tenderness

Published by DREAMSPINNER PRESS
http://www.dreamspinnerpress.com

# Truth & Tenderness

TERE MICHAELS

Published by
DREAMSPINNER PRESS

5032 Capital Circle SW, Suite 2, PMB# 279, Tallahassee, FL 32305-7886 USA
http://www.dreamspinnerpress.com/

Truth & Tenderness
© 2015 Tere Michaels.

Cover Art
© 2015 Aaron Anderson.
aaronbydesign55@gmail.com.
Cover content is for illustrative purposes only and any person depicted on the cover is a model.

ISBN: 978-1-63216-710-1
Digital ISBN: 978-1-63216-711-8
Library of Congress Control Number: 2014921686
First Edition May 2015

Printed in the United States of America
∞
This paper meets the requirements of
ANSI/NISO Z39.48-1992 (Permanence of Paper).

# Acknowledgments

This has been a long journey—seven years since their story started and twice that from the time that Matt and Evan (and Jim and Griffin) first appeared in my thoughts, and I couldn't have come this far without the tireless support of friends and family.

Thank you to my husband and son, who've always been so proud and supportive: thank you.

Thank you to my family and friends, who read a gay romance for the first time just because my name was on it: thank you.

Thank you to my fellow writers, who've celebrated my success, urged me through the dark days, and recommended my work like it was their job: thank you.

Thank you to my editors and publishers and cover artists and publicity folks: thank you for your amazing work.

Thank you to my fans—what can I say? Your fierce love (and irritation) for these characters has been a revelation and a dream come true. To invoke passion, to stimulate the creation of actual feelings for fictional characters—it's what every writer dreams of doing when they sit down with that blank sheet of paper. Thanks, from the bottom of my heart.

This one's for you.

# Prologue

EVAN FIXED his tie in the mirror, smoothing imaginary wrinkles from the dark material as he tucked it into his jacket. Out of the corner of his eye, he caught sight of his hat sitting on the bed, the last piece of his dress blues to put on.

Today it began.

His captaincy with the New York City Police Department.

The swearing-in ceremony at 1 Police Plaza was scheduled to begin in two hours. Downstairs, his family waited—and fidgeted—in their good going-out clothes, with cameras and cell phones ready for his descent. Their raucous laughter and conversation drifted through the door. They were loud and obnoxious, and he had no doubt they were practicing wolf whistles for when he was announced.

He loved them so much.

But yeah. Evan Cerelli, captain of Midtown South.

A box of things collected and forgotten sat on the emptied desk of his new command; a selection of pictures—updated and carefully chosen—waited downstairs in his workbag. Tomorrow at eight in the morning, he would conduct a meeting of senior officers to discuss the current temperature and immediate necessities of the quiet precinct.

Evan swallowed, smoothed back imaginary unruly hairs of his salt-and-pepper military haircut.

From rookie on a beat to captain, a twenty-plus-year career shaping into a life he couldn't even have imagined. He remembered his first swearing-in ceremony when he graduated from the Academy. Sherri and the little girls by his side, their shining and happy faces as he became a member of the NYPD. Sitting across from them at lunch, sharing a tender look with his beautiful wife. Grateful for a job with good pay and great benefits so he could take care of the three people he loved most in the world.

Evan couldn't have predicted today. Any of it.

He blinked at his reflection, a blip in time of a different day, a different room, a different solemn outfit. That was an ending, a painful life-changing agony that he wasn't sure he could survive, and this—this was his next new beginning.

Touched by nostalgia, Evan bypassed the hat and went for the small wooden box tucked behind the ceramic lamp on top of his tall dresser. It held three rings: a large gold band, and the smaller matching one with the delicate engagement ring returned to him by the coroner. He brought the box out of the shadows and into the light from the lamp. Easy to remember putting those rings on Sherri's finger, the cool slide of the metal as she put on his.

And then the slide off, the decision that while he'd always love his wife, their marriage was in the past and being with Matt was the present.

The future.

Evan's throat tightened. He'd long made peace with the minefield of loving two people so absolutely. The life he lived now didn't feel like a substitute or settling—Evan had taken the hand dealt to him by circumstances, done his best, learned from his mistakes.

Learned as best he could.

Nothing was perfect, but it felt good.

He brushed his fingertips over the rings, tracing each before shutting the box, and then returned it to its rightful place. Hat in hand, he took one more look in the full-length mirror, from shiny shoes to the faint gray mixed among the darkness of his buzz cut. The mantle of captaincy—the family waiting for him, waiting to celebrate this day.

Evan Cerelli took a deep breath, then went to join his family downstairs.

# Chapter 1

"DAAAAD!" KATIE yelled, checking her watch with an exaggerated toe-tapping annoyance Matt knew she got from living with him the past few years. The living room was packed with five Cerelli children, Kent the significant other, plus their extended family, Helena and Shane, and the air had started to get a bit ripe.

"I'm turning on the air-conditioning," Danny said as he walked by. Matt didn't try to stop him even as Miranda balked.

"It's still winter!" Fortunately her boyfriend, Kent, was there to wrap his arms around her with an accompanying coo.

"Too many people in the house, not enough air." Matt glanced at his reflection on the TV screen—off, for once; he didn't think it had that setting—one last time.

"Am I taking pictures?" Helena asked, even as her husband, Shane, gently removed the expensive camera from her hands.

"No, sweetheart."

They made an interesting couple, Shane in his snazzy tan suit and jade green tie—and a haircut that probably cost $150—and Helena in her dress blues, pin neat and pulled together. Something about the uniform made Matt melancholy, no doubt the tip of the iceberg before a day spent at 1 Police Plaza, in a sea of blue, with waves of memories washing over him.

And now all the water metaphors were making him need to take a piss.

"Daaaaaaad!" Katie yelled again.

A door slammed overhead; then the clatter of footsteps began. Shane angled himself like a paparazzo at the bottom of the staircase, jostling against Katie like he was jockeying for best position.

It escalated quickly, the neat row of Cerelli children school photos shaking against the wall.

"Oh God, the pictures are going to be blurry," Miranda huffed from behind them.

The mock fighting stopped as Evan stepped into view—and Matt let a flirty wolf whistle fly. The blush on his boyfriend's cheeks made it even more worthwhile.

"Wow," Matt said, low and as sexy as he was capable of making his voice.

Evan smirked as Matt easily pushed his way between Shane and Katie, then closed the distance between them. "Like something you see?" Evan asked quietly.

But not quietly enough, because retching noises began behind them, led by Helena.

As Evan paused on the last step, Matt ignored them all, sweeping an arm around Evan's middle.

"Whatever dirty thing you're going to say, shut up," Evan muttered as he leaned down to kiss Matt on the mouth—quick, fleeting, but sweet enough to make Matt behave.

"Oh, that's a nice shot. That's the cover of our Christmas card right there," Katie said loudly as Elizabeth giggled.

Evan leaned around Matt's embrace. "Can we start making our way out to the car? We'll take pictures after the ceremony."

"Yes, sir!" That was Helena. Then all the kids echoed her sarcastically, even Miranda and Kent.

"They're not moving, are they?" Matt asked, sneaking his hand down to pinch Evan's ass under his jacket.

"No," Evan answered as the corners of his mouth began to twitch.

"I got this."

Matt moved quickly because he knew Evan knew what he was going to do—Matt wasn't subtle. Ever.

Matt surged up to plant a wicked kiss on Evan's mouth—tongue, a bitten lip. It sounded wet and dirty, and from the squeals behind him, it looked it too. The door slammed a few seconds later, the hooting and hollering trailing behind the kids a second after.

Evan pulled away, finally. His mouth looked lush and gorgeous, his eyes were a little unfocused, and a faint hint of perspiration was forming at his hairline.

And at some point, he'd dropped his hat.

"That cleared the room," Evan said, a tiny bit out of breath.

"We'll have to remember that after we get back from the ceremony," Matt said with a smirk, so wicked that Evan shook his head.

"The uniform, right?"

"Well, it helps that you're wearing it and I'm specifically tuned to want to jump you in any and all clothing." Matt adopted a solemn expression. "That's probably a good thing, or this could be an especially uncomfortable ceremony in a room with that much blue polyester." The joking helped, even if Evan's face was doing that painfully sympathetic thing.

So Matt kissed him again, bringing one hand up to touch his face gently.

The gesture said, *I'm fine*.

Evan took a deep breath as he came up for air. He nodded, his gaze never leaving Matt's face.

That said, *I know*.


THEY TOOK three vehicles to 1 Police Plaza, Evan checking his watch the entire time. Matt felt validated with his "you kids go in one car, we'll go in another" being a good call. He knew his boyfriend, and he knew the freaking out hadn't reached full capacity yet.

"We're good. We're early. Calm down," Matt soothed, following the slow-moving traffic toward the nearest parking garage. Three blocks away and he'd already made a reservation online—not to mention he'd purposely gotten everyone out of the house forty minutes early.

His phone beeped and Evan reached into the center console to read the text.

"Jim is already here," he read.

Matt put on his blinker and waited for an opening in the traffic to pull into the entrance of the underground parking. A guy in an orange vest across the street was waving at him frantically with his flag.

"I bet you Jim got here an hour ago."

Evan read the text again, then laughed as he dropped the phone. "Ninety minutes."

Jim Shea, Matt's old friend and now security company partner, had made the drive down from Dutchess County to help them celebrate. His fiancé, Griffin, was away in Los Angeles finishing up production on a movie, so Matt and Evan were making sure Jim got fed and watered properly in his absence.

While they weren't the best of friends, Evan had grown comfortable with Jim's presence in their lives. And Evan adored Griffin, Jim's fiancé—who, in turn, adored trying to make Evan sputter in public—and the jealousy he'd felt over Jim and Matt's one-time affair had dissipated.

Slowly.

"Griffin sent me a very nice e-card with a rude joke in it," Evan commented as Matt finally put Orange Vest Guy out of his misery and pulled in, followed by the second SUV, driven by Miranda, and then Shane and Helena's kicky Fiat.

"I would expect nothing else."

"He also sent a gift with Jim, but apparently I'm not allowed to open it until we're alone."

Matt fist-pumped as he parked the car at the bottom of the ramp. "Woo-hoo, sex toys!"

"Oh my God."


THE ENTRANCE of 1 Police Plaza, predictably, held a slow-moving line to security. Their sprawling group got ID'd and searched eventually, with everyone seeming to have been bitten by the same jittering bug of nerves at the same time. Evan gave each of the family a kiss (except Kent and Shane, though the latter asked nicely) and then dashed to the stage. Matt watched him go with a ridiculous smile on his face.

"Ugh, so gross," Katie said, dreamy and delighted, as she looped her arm around his.

His favorite Cerelli child on one arm and the two youngest accounted for—Danny shadowing Helena and Shane and Elizabeth stuck to Miranda's side—Matt led everyone to the auditorium.

Jim was "by the flags" and saving a row; even with the crush of humanity excitedly filling seats, Matt felt confident Jim's glare would keep interlopers away.

He was right.

In his own Seattle PD dress blues, retired detective Jim Shea cut quite the distinguished figure. Several ladies were checking him out without even bothering to hide it, and at least two rookies tripped on a stripe in the rug walking by.

Matt couldn't hide his grin when he caught Jim's attention.

"Hey, Officer Stud. If you had a boom box, everyone would think you were the entertainment," Matt teased as Jim stood to give him a hug.

"Jackass." Jim punched him in the arm as they separated. He exchanged pleasantries with the kids, Shane, and Helena; then everyone played musical chairs for the best view.

Shane sat on the end, Katie by his side, as professional photographers for the day. Miranda put Elizabeth on her lap so the petite teen could see over the tall people in front of them, while Danny slouched as he played with his phone.

Matt and Jim sat on the other end, Matt flipping through Jim's program to find Evan's name. Two other captains were getting moved up today, and a half-a-dozen speeches were on the agenda as well.

Boring. He might join Danny and disappear into his phone for a while.

A bit of jostling about ten rows ahead caught his eye.

The press.

More press than usual for this sort of thing, a fact that most people in attendance wouldn't realize. Matt gave Jim an elbow to his side, gesturing with a chin raise toward the people setting up cameras and microphones.

"Oh," Jim said.

They didn't say anything out loud. Elizabeth and Danny were in earshot, and who knew what gossips were hanging around behind them.

Today was interesting beyond the usual buried picture and a few inches of copy. From today on, an openly gay captain would serve in the NYPD.

"He's gonna flip," Jim murmured as Matt sighed, tugging at his tie.


EVAN SECURED his hat backstage, breathing in and out as people flitted around him. They were about to start, and he couldn't fight the growing sense of worry. He didn't like being on display, particularly if it meant calling attention to himself for reasons less than important in his mind. A promotion felt good, but Evan felt much more proud of lives saved than shiny squares on his uniform. This was a course of action that would put him in the spotlight—for things not entirely related to his record.

For most captains, that light swung to big cases and political hot topics that might fall into their laps.

The attention would be on Evan for an entirely different reason.

"Evan?"

He turned at the sound of his name, coming face to face with a welcome sight: Casper Vaughn, a friend from GOAL—the LGBT police organization—and a bit of relief from the strangers swarming about.

"Casper, hi," he said, shaking his hand. "What are you doing back here?"

"PR liaison." Casper gestured toward the badge on the lapel of his expensive navy suit. "I'm moving over to Midtown South." The smile on his face was wide and grew wider as Evan realized what that meant.

"Thank God," Evan muttered.

Casper laughed, clapping one hand on his shoulder. "You'll be fine. I'll take care of you."

"Why'd they move you over from…," Evan started then clamped his mouth closed. Oh, right.

"It's fine with me. I like the idea of trailblazing our way through Midtown South. You and I are on the front line."

"Of matinee traffic jams and street closures due to filming," he said dryly.

Casper, who always looked like he was ready to step in front of a camera, reminded him of an even more polished version of Shane. A Harvard-educated beach bum. Older, broader, but still brimming with charm and direct eye contact that eventually made you want to blush a little. When he winked and leaned in like he was sharing a secret, Evan wasn't surprised by the intrusion into his personal space.

"With your authoritative presence and my ceaseless sparkle, we are going to make such a great team, they'll be moving us somewhere better in no time."

Of course Casper saw that as a good thing. Evan, on the other hand, knew that meant more serious crime, more victims, more intensity, and making statements in the middle of chaos and anger. But he didn't pop Casper's balloon just yet.

"I'm counting on you not to let me make a fool of myself," Evan said with a smile, ducking back a half step. Casper's aftershave had started to tickle his nose.

"No worries, Evan. I'm going to make you look great." That wide smile stayed in place, even as Evan heard someone calling in the distance that they were ready to get started.

"Are you coming to the reception afterward with Tony?" Evan asked, readjusting his hat.

A somber veil fell over Casper's expression. "No. Uh, Tony moved back to Chicago two weeks ago."

Evan stopped mid-wrinkle-inspection. He'd seen them—last month? At the GOAL fundraising meeting?—and everything seemed fine between Casper and his friendly partner, who worked for an advertising agency in midtown.

"What?"

"Tony and I split up. I haven't really told anyone." Casper looked around, clearly uncomfortable. "It wasn't pretty," he said with a grimace. "It's been eleven years, you know? How do you make that announcement?"

Evan had no clue, because when he'd experienced a breakup like that—breaking up with Matt all those years ago—he'd told no one, not until those horrible few weeks nearly knocked the last bit of life out of him. And then only because his depressive grief threatened to derail his entire life, a fact his friends and his boss at the time couldn't overlook as he fell apart. Evan just hadn't been able to hide it anymore.

Evan knew what it felt like to miss someone so badly you thought it might actually kill you.

"I'm so sorry," Evan murmured, moving closer to Casper, touching his arm gently. "For both of you."

Casper's pale blue eyes got shiny, but he threw that smile back into place and hitched his shoulders back into perfect posture once again. "Thanks."

"Cas...."

"No, it's—I'm sorry, I shouldn't be getting into this right now. This is your big moment, and I know your whole family is out there waiting to see you sworn in."

The brief stutter in Casper's expression was worse than tears, but Evan also understood stoicism in the face of emotion because you knew damn well if you started, you weren't ever going to stop.

"Find us at the reception. You have a lot of friends out there. I'm sure everyone would be glad to see you," Evan said.

"We'll see. And anyway, you and I will be getting a lot of time together come tomorrow."

Evan nodded and gave Casper a little salute before heading over to where a woman in a headset was lining people up.

Time to become Captain Evan Cerelli.

# Chapter 2

MATT LEANED back in the comfortable leather chair, letting it creak against his weight. It was "his" chair, for when he made the drive up to work with Jim in his fancy-schmancy garage office. Most folks might just throw some yard sale finds in a concrete-walled bunker, but no, Jim had money and people who knew how to spend it.

And it showed.

The walls were painted a rustic tan, with stylish black curtains on the two windows. One looked out at the tree-laden property and the other faced the pool and patio. When the weather was nice, Matt brought the twins up and let them loose on the understated luxury of upscale rural living, which meant they sat in the pool or the hot tub until he had to bribe them to get in the car. The furniture—from the huge overstuffed leather couch to the matching recliners and vintage tables—begged you to stay a few hours more. Work, nap. Catch a game on the huge screen on the far wall.

Plus the double-wide stainless-steel fridge over in the house always appeared full, as if by magic, tempting Matt's stomach and luring him away from his desk at times other than Jim's enforced lunch hour.

"You know the rules, young man," Jim would say as Matt threw a vintage throw pillow in the shape of a pug at his head.

Today Matt and Jim were working on end-of-the-month billing and their schedule for the rest of March. "All the invoices are out, we have the installations scheduled." Jim thumbed through a stack of papers from the middle of their shared desk, which was the approximate size of Matt's old studio apartment.

"Wow, we're efficient."

"I'm efficient. You charm people into giving us business," Jim pointed out, placing the papers into the wire basket marked "completed" in his neat block handwriting.

"The perfect team." Matt righted the chair, reaching onto the desk to get his phone. No new alerts or messages—all was right back down in Brooklyn, apparently. Evan, in full captain mode, was rarely home before nine, and the twins were midway through their freshman year of high school, piles of homework keeping them busy when they were home and not out doing sports or color guard. Once Matt fulfilled his duties in purchasing food, paying bills, and leaving cash out for the kids, he was free to roam.

Which generally meant up to Jim's house.

"Next up."

Matt sighed. "Lunch?"

"It's eleven thirty!"

"By the time you're finished setting up the spread and pouring me a beer...."

"You're ridiculous," Jim said, but he was laughing as he stood up. "Okay, I'll see what Georgia left us. But you have to start working on the camera layout for Bennett's new offices."

"Fine, fine." Matt lifted the lid of Jim's laptop, waking the beast within. "Do we think he works for the CIA and all this movie and stage stuff is his deep cover?"

"No." Jim made it to the door, then paused to shrug on his jacket against the early spring chill. "Maybe."

"And then he could make a movie about him making movies while he was in the CIA." Matt knocked on his head like it was a ripe coconut. "Tell Griffin this. I'll split the profits with him."

"Griffin. Griffin. Right. Guy with the tall hair and squinty eyes," Jim said dryly. "I have his picture on the fridge so I don't forget what he looks like."

It was said lightheartedly, but then Jim ducked out, the wind and light rain rattling the walls until he slammed the door behind him.

Maybe not so much a joke anymore.

Matt didn't mind driving up to Dutchess County to work at Jim's place. At first it seemed better to have him down to Matt's home office in Brooklyn—it was comfortable and he could stay for dinner if it got too late. But quickly Matt clued in to the fact that all the domestic bliss (even if it was two teenagers and the fleeting appearance of Evan) just brought him down even further.

So Matt took the train or hopped in the car to keep Jim company at his house.

He poked around the neatly organized folders on Jim's laptop. Things were painstakingly labeled, color coded, and there wasn't a single cute icon in sight. Even the background was a solemn blue-gray field.

Matt knew how to replace that with a kitten, and he put it on his to-do list.

Click, click, search. He found Bennett's folder and all the subfolders beyond. The Ames family was his business's sugar daddy, and it showed in the range of dates listed, of all the jobs he'd done for them. Matt scrolled down until he found "Bryant Park Office ReOrg" and clicked on it.

He didn't know what he did wrong, but the program decided to quit, Matt cursing the whole time until he could click through the whole "no, I don't want to report it, just give me the damn file." He went to Recently Opened on the menu and thought he clicked the right folder.

But what popped up wasn't the office specs for Bennett's new place. It was a collection of clippings.

Matt leaned in.

Crime scenes. Reports. Notes typed in blocks between the official documents. SCHOOL SCHEDULE. CONFIRM HE WAS ON TRIP.

Maps of the West Coast.

Coroner's reports from almost ten years ago.

Then? A name.

TRIPP INGERSOLL.

He didn't need to go further. Matt knew exactly what this was.

Every cop—on the force, retired, hooked up to machines prolonging the months—had one of these. Their white whale, the case that just wouldn't leave them alone.

The ones you lost. The ones you never solved. The faces that came with you after you retired.

Tripp Ingersoll, rich college kid accused of killing a teenaged hooker in LA. A jury that wanted to believe someone with so much going for him wouldn't do something so horrible, so he'd been walking free the past few years, much to Jim's horror.

Then Jim made his white whale a cop's worst mistake: he became emotionally involved with the dead girl's parents.

Matt clicked the little *X* on the corner of the document, somber. He didn't bother to open the other file; he just got up and grabbed his jacket, then headed over to the house.

JIM WAS leaning against the counter when Matt walked in, texting with Griffin in Los Angeles.

*When are you coming home?*

*Tuesday.*

*It's Wednesday.*

*I know. I'm sorry. But Tuesday.*

*Jim?*

*I know, okay? Maybe you can come here?*

*Jim? Jesus, come on. I can't do this again.*

*I'll see if I can come out for the weekend.*

*THANK YOU. I love you.*

*I love you too.*

Jim tossed his phone onto a stack of mail and magazines waiting for Griffin's return. Everything in the house felt like someone had hit Pause.

Hold off on wedding plans.

Wait to redo the guest bathroom.

Don't make an appointment with the rug guy just yet.

Fly three thousand miles to get five or six hours of your fiancé's free time. Sex to reconnect and sleeping in each other's arms to pretend nothing was strained and exhausting.

Matt was still standing by the back door, and Jim reluctantly drew himself out of the pity party to look at his friend.

And then he wanted to look away because of the gravity of Matt's expression.

THEY SAT in the living room, posh and comfortable in tans and blues. They had sandwiches and pasta salad, courtesy of the housekeeper, and beers—two apiece—on coasters.

"I didn't throw away my notes after the trial," Jim said eventually, concentrating on the turkey on rye on his plate. "Then one day you get bored. You start thinking," he murmured. "You think you're going to do just one search, just to satisfy the curiosity, but you keep putting his name in that little box and suddenly it's three hours later. Then it's three days, and then…"

"Then it's three years later. Got it," Matt answered. He put his half-cleaned plate down on the coffee table, then leaned toward Jim, elbows on his knees. "I've been there. Haven't been a cop in years, but I still think about the ones we never closed." His voice was soft and full of pity; Jim blinked but said nothing. "But the case is over. Even if you find anything—double jeopardy."

"I know that." It came out snappy, even as Jim tried to rein in his bubbling anger. He knew—logic was his tether; it kept him sane and alive. "I know. He's never going to go down for Carmen's murder. But…."

"You think it wasn't his first."

Jim dropped his plate on the table, then sank back into the easy give of the sofa. He wanted to kick something, throw a chair through the big picture window on the other side of the room. When tracking Tripp's life was a dirty little secret, he could still pretend it was insane, an exercise in frivolity. Exposing it to the real world, to another person, made it a mission. Made it possible. He wanted to *ruin* something in this moment of conflicted anger—he just didn't want it to be his life.

If word got out he was trying to find another case to pin on Tripp Ingersoll, the fallout wouldn't affect just him.

Griffin's movie would be a magnet for bad press. All his hard work—and the memories of Ed, Delia, and Carmen Kelly—would be dragged through the muddy rehash.

He'd lose the endlessly dragged-on civil case Tripp had against him and the Seattle PD.

He didn't care about money, but he sure as hell cared about his reputation.

And his fiancé's. And the Kelly family's.

"You know what I'm about to say." Matt spoke with such seriousness in his tone that Jim couldn't even look at him. His face burned with embarrassment.

"I know."

"The risks, Jim."

"I know!"

"Terrific. You know. You get it. You're not stupid," Matt said sternly. "Now do something about it."

Jim leaned back to stare at the ceiling. Skylights showed the steady mist outside, beading against the glass. "I'll delete it."

"Jim."

A warning word. From the first moment they had met, Jim knew Matt had his number. They had each other's numbers. Platitudes weren't going to work.

Jim opened his mouth, because he was going to say, *You're right, I'll delete it and forget about him,* but he knew that was a lie. For all the rationality and knowing better, Jim couldn't forget Carmen on that slab or her parents in side-by-side graves with her within two years of her death. Carmen's blood was on Tripp Ingersoll's hands, but sometimes Jim felt like Delia's and Ed's blood were on his.

"I need to finish this. I need to see if there's anything out there. And if there's not, if he's clean—" Jim choked on the word. "—I'll get rid of everything."

Matt sighed dramatically. "Right." Another sigh. "I'll help you out— we can put in a few hours during the week. It'll go faster that way."

Jim sat up slowly, unfolding his tightly held limbs as he moved to look at Matt. Every cell of his body buzzed with permission from Matt to pursue this, permission to be obsessed and channel his energy into something potentially meaningful. It was like a fucking gift.

"What? This way I can keep an eye on you, make sure you don't end up doing something stupid." Matt leaned back in the chair, folding his hands over his stomach. "But if we don't find anything...."

Jim put his hand up. "Then it's done."

Matt scrutinized him like he might a perp. Jim knew that expression. "Then it's done."

Jim's response was an approving smile.

MATT DROVE back to the city, taking the winding country roads slowly in the bad weather. Two texts from Elizabeth came through before he left Jim's house; the first said she was staying at her friend Star's house for dinner so they could work on a project, followed by news that Danny had gone to the varsity baseball practice at the batting cage to "hang out."

No word from Evan, which meant he'd be home late. Probably another meeting with Casper, a name he was already tired of hearing from his boyfriend's mouth.

So Matt drove slower because there wasn't a reason to hurry.

Jim's obsession with Tripp Ingersoll poked at him, dragged him through his own memory bank. On the force, he had felt an all-consuming need to close his cases—every single one of them, no matter if the victim was innocent or anything but.

He wanted to have an ending.

He wanted to know his efforts led to justice.

He wanted the badge to mean something all the time, for each case.

It cost him his badge in the end.

The rain beat down on the windshield, obscuring his view. Matt slowed down a little more, caught in a swamp of memories.

# Chapter 3

GRIFFIN DRAKE walked on shaky legs from the idling sedan in the driveway to the house. Whatever the thing past utter exhaustion was, well, he felt about two weeks of no sleep past that. The movie had wrapped, the postproduction was underway, and Griffin could finally go home.

At three thirty in the morning.

He vaguely registered the car pulling away, focused intently on the front door with its cheery pussy willow wreath that clearly wasn't the work of his fiancé.

Shivering in the night air, Griffin dropped his carry-on and suitcase on the front steps. He needed both hands to fumble with the key and lock, taking three tries to get his fingers to cooperate.

On try number four, the tumblers clicked and the door opened.

Jim, framed in the doorway and backlit with the foyer chandelier, smiled down at him, and Griffin tried not to burst into hysterics. Tears or laughter—he had no idea which would come out if he opened his mouth.

"Like the first time we met," he managed before Jim reached out and pulled him into the house—and his arms.

"Luggage," Griffin said against his chest, but Jim—big, silent, beautiful Jim, whose hands felt like a gift on Griffin's body—manhandled him through the foyer and into the living room and then down on the couch.

"I'll get it. Just relax, okay?" he murmured as Griffin sprawled back on the pillows and throw blanket on the long couch. Griffin realized a second later that Jim had been waiting for him here.

"Oh God." Griffin closed his eyes and let the sound of Jim moving back to get his bags soothe him. He was here, and Jim was here, and all the distance was almost over.

Griffin woke with a start, jumping a little when he opened his eyes and realized he was home and not in a hotel room or the near-empty loft. He sat up slowly, running both hands through his wrecked hair as he twisted the kinks out of his back. It took a minute, but he realized his clothes—save his underwear and socks—were gone, the air toasty warm and the blanket from their bed laid over his legs.

And the sun was out.

"Jim?" Griffin called quietly. He moved the blanket as he swung his legs over the side of the couch.

A sound from the direction of the kitchen drew Griffin to the other side of the house.

In their gourmet kitchen—domain of the housekeeper unless you counted putting leftovers away as cooking—Jim stood over the stovetop, poking at something in a frying pan.

Griffin slid his socked feet over the smooth wood floor, making as little noise as possible. He admired Jim's strong shoulders and muscular legs, currently on display in an outfit of gym shorts and a tank top. He revisited the back of his fiancé's neck, so excellently built for nuzzling or biting, depending on what Griffin was doing back there.

Nothing about Jim had changed since they met—at least not on the outside. No, it was the revelations of who he was on the inside that made Griffin's insides flutter.

"You're just standing there staring at my ass," Jim said suddenly. Griffin jumped at the sound. "I feel cheap," Jim added, not turning around.

"Actually I was thinking about your big heart and super-smart brain, but now I'm thinking about your monstrous ego."

Griffin wandered over to slip his arms around Jim's waist and bury his face against that fabulous patch of skin. "Thank you for taking care of me last night," he murmured, dropping kisses between words. The smell of eggs and bacon wafted up to his nose.

"Are you grinding up against me because you missed me or because you smell breakfast?" Jim asked dryly.

"Um—I love you?"

They both laughed and Griffin's exhausted disorientation lifted a bit more; making the movie had been an amazing opportunity, but God, he was just glad to be here, in this moment.

THEY ATE in the dining room once Jim moved the stacks of books, mail, and tile samples to the opposite end so they had room to put their plates.

"Do I want to know?" Griffin asked, fork poised and expression wary.

"Your mail, we need another bookcase, and Daisy said you have to pick tile for the bathroom," Jim recited obediently. He ripped his slice of toast in half, then began transferring half the jar of apple butter to its crispy surface. Nirvana.

"Right. Crap." Griffin sighed as he shoved some of his scrambled eggs in his mouth.

Jim watched him chew, then reach for the hot sauce. "Eggs should not be spicy."

"Spicy is debatable but taste is not."

"Fine. Last time I make you breakfast." He defiantly put another layer of apple butter on his apple butter.

"Salt is not a spice, James."

Jim's scowl became hard to maintain as Griffin began to trail his foot up his bare leg under the table.

THEY LEFT the dirty plates on the dining room table, which was how Griffin knew Jim had reached a state of "sex-starved" that overruled all his other functions. On the couch, Griffin pushed Jim down among the blanket and pillows and cushions, dropping to his knees between the V of his fiancé's legs.

"I missed you so much," Griffin murmured, rubbing his hands up and down the furred length of Jim's thighs, dipping under the leg of his shorts.

The tense muscles, the mouthwatering bulge pressing against the seam of Jim's shorts—Griffin made a little sound of want as he leaned down, breathing in the scent of masculine arousal, nuzzling against the inside of Jim's thigh.

"Stop playing," Jim whispered, hands on his waistband. Griffin looked up to see the sheen of sweat on his fiancé's face, the way he trembled as he lifted his hips and began to push his shorts down.

Griffin moaned as he grabbed a handful of cotton and helped divest Jim of his shorts. They didn't even get them entirely off—the shorts hung off Jim's knee, as Griffin couldn't wait to get his mouth around Jim's straining cock.

The sound Jim made as his dick hit the back of Griffin's throat unraveled something desperate in him. He was home, Jim was his, and everything was going to be all right.


AFTER THIRTY-SIX hours of reconnecting with Jim, Griffin felt ready to turn his phone back on.

Only 111 texts, e-mails, and voice mails. He considered himself lucky.

On the ride to Manhattan, Jim drove and Griffin managed his life on his smartphone. He tried to chat with Jim at the same time, keenly aware of the growing tension from the driver's seat.

"Almost done," he said cheerfully. "Just a few more."

He forwarded things, delegated, demurred, and delayed. Anything he wanted to brag about died on his tongue; Griffin didn't miss the irony that the case that had brought him to the love of his life was currently opening a valley of strain between them.

"Gosh, I'm so glad to be back on the East Coast," Griffin enthused, answering yet another question for the movie's media coordinator. "All that lousy sun was giving me a headache."

Jim made a sound of agreement. Or he was being attacked by a bat.

Griffin snuck a look. No bats.

"We have a ton of stuff to do, so I hope your schedule is clear. Wedding plans, of course, and let's just get that bathroom done," he rambled. "Maybe spend a weekend at my dad's house?"

"He's in Atlantic City next weekend with Dotty. Then he has that reunion thing with his friends from high school in Maine," Jim said, changing lanes as they sped toward the city.

"Oh."

Jim knew his father's schedule better than he did. Also…. "Who's Dotty?"

JIM HAD the pleasure of explaining to Griffin that his long-widowed father was now dating a woman named Dotty, who owned a yarn store in the next town over—and he had actually been dating her for almost two years. Dating her with carnal relations being had, that was for damn sure. The sisters didn't know yet, and Jim demurred from taking on that responsibility.

Eight women, one father's girlfriend—he didn't have riot gear anymore.

"Oh."

It was the only thing Griffin said for the next twenty minutes.

JIM PARKED in the underground garage of the Midtown building where Bennett Ames's new offices were housed. The view of Bryant Park—gorgeous. The proximity to great restaurants and all the city had to offer—obvious and generous.

The need to move offices yet again, including a full renovation?

Well, Jim had no clue.

While the money filled the coffers of his and Matt's business, he didn't see the point. There was some story about being close to the theater where Bennett's latest production had found a home, but frankly Jim thought that was bullshit.

Whatever. Not his money.

Griffin finally finished his business on the phone and the thing disappeared into his pocket—something Jim was grateful for. Throwing it out the window while they went over the Tappan Zee Bridge seemed like the best idea he'd ever had at the time.

"So I'm going to have this meeting with Bennett; then we're all going to lunch," Griffin said for the eleventh time. The Dotty story had clearly left him flustered as he fussed with his hair in the side mirror.

"I know. I brought a book to read to fill my lonely hours," Jim said lightly, but Griffin straightened up and gave him an awkward look over the hood of the car. "So you can take as long as you need," he added.

Griffin nodded and then walked toward the garage elevator.

Okay, then.

Jim caught up with him in two quick strides and slid his hand into Griffin's, linking their fingers together.

They didn't talk, but Jim couldn't help noticing Griffin holding on for dear life.


JIM HAD indeed brought a book: the new Dan Brown in paperback, a grocery receipt for a bookmark somewhere in the middle. Griffin's heart fluttered as he leaned over to drop a kiss on Jim's mouth.

"I love you," Griffin said, taking the smile Jim rewarded him with all the way back to Bennett's office.

Of course everything was gorgeously decorated, masculine and bold, with a view of the park that looked straight out of a movie. Bennett greeted him from behind a parson's table, looking like a supermodel in tight blue jeans and a lightweight V-neck sweater.

"Welcome home," Bennett said as he gave Griffin a hug. "How are you doing?"

"It's weird—I kinda feel like an astronaut that just returned to earth. How was that my life once upon a time?" Griffin sat down in one of the two wing chairs in front of Bennett's desk.

Bennett dropped into the chair next to him.

"Well, your life is here on the East Coast now, and unless that changes...."

Griffin was already shaking his head. "No. I want to be here."

"Wonderful."

They chatted for a bit about Daisy (considering another play) and Sadie (walking and talking and eating like a champ) and then dove into the postmortem on the movie's production. All of Griffin's fears about his first producing job, his carefully and lovingly crafted script, began to melt away as Bennett went on a spree of praise and congratulations.

Test audiences were being booked, music and effects were almost finished, the media campaign was revving up. It was finally going to happen.

Griffin's heart beat like a wild drum in his chest. "Thank you for this opportunity—" he started, but Bennett cut him off.

"No. Don't thank me. You did a wonderful job—everyone had something positive to say. I should be thanking you for adding another person to my community of creative friends," he added, winking as Griffin blushed.

How different a working relationship from when he worked for Claus, Daisy's first husband and a supreme asshole.

"Well, if you need anything else," joked Griffin.

Bennett's grin got wider. "Actually, I was thinking you might want to take a look at some old projects that I haven't had a chance to develop."

Griffin blinked. "What?"

"I have properties I purchased with the hope of doing something, but life got in the way and some really amazing stories got lost in the bottom of the filing cabinet. How'd you like a shot at them?"

"To... produce?"

"Yeah. You'll have to take a promotion, though." Bennett laughed, tipping his head back. "God, Griffin—your face."

"Never play poker with me."

"Actually, I should—I'd make a fortune."

The meeting concluded with a strapping fair-haired young intern named Lars bringing Griffin a file box stacked with folders and scripts.

"Not yet converted to digital file. My apologies," Bennett said as Lars put the box on the leather sofa in the corner.

"No, no, it's fine. I'd rather read them this way anyway." Griffin ran his fingers over the box like they held a treasure. Because maybe they did. Maybe he could find another gem in all the noise, something he loved and wanted to bring to the world.

Maybe he could find another piece of his career puzzle.

Bennett dismissed Lars, who did a sauntering runway model thing that Griffin noticed (he was engaged, not dead) and then noticed that Bennett did as well.

A little hum of concern niggled at Griffin's brain, but before he could speak, the door opened again.

Daisy and Sadie entered wearing matching pink floral dresses and identical bright smiles, and Bennett's attention became entirely focused on his "most beautiful girls."

A second later, smothered with hugs and kisses from his best friend and his goddaughter, Griffin's fleeting concern was lost to the best kind of distraction.

THEY ATE in a private dining room at the Bryant Park Grill, devouring lobsters and Israeli couscous and a few bottles of wine. Jim smiled at least two genuine smiles—Griffin counted—and everything felt right.

Daisy fed Sadie mashed sweet potatoes and sautéed spinach. The toddler cooperated about 50 percent of the time—the rest she devoted to playing peekaboo with her adoring godfather. Griffin let the "adult" conversation drift away, concentrating on the little girl and her charming grin as he ducked behind his raised linen napkin.

Sadie didn't tire of the game and neither did Griffin. He'd missed her terribly. She was another on a long list of people he wanted to see more often, and not over FaceTime on his phone between meetings. Once upon a time, he'd lived three thousand miles away from everyone he loved except Daisy—a different Daisy, a brittle and self-absorbed woman who barely resembled the happy sprite with the pixie cut who was wiping down a dirty toddler without blinking.

Now—now he was tired of being away. Tired of Hollywood and living alone. Tired of things that took his attention away from his family.

Sadie was his family. Sadie was a representation of so much.

When Jim slid his hand onto Griffin's leg and took his hand, Griffin swallowed hard and blinked.

Sadie was a symbol of what he really wanted.

# Chapter 4

"EVAN?"

Up to eyeballs in paper, Evan didn't even look up when he heard his name. There wasn't much urgency in the tone, so he let himself finish reading the last paragraph of the report before turning his attention to...

Casper Vaughn.

Evan smiled. This was the right kind of distraction. "Hey."

Casper walked into the office and shut the door behind him, silencing the mild chatter of the squad room. Evan pushed his work to one side as Casper sat down.

"How goes the dynamic world of Midtown South?" Casper asked, a smirk teasing at his lips.

Evan gestured at the files on his desk. "I have signed my name three hundred times today and it's not even two in the afternoon. What do you think?"

Casper covered his mouth with his hand, smothering a cough/laugh in an entirely unconvincing way.

"Tomorrow I have two luncheons to attend and a meeting about excessive horn honking in the Garment District. There are talking points. About excessive honking."

"Riveting." Casper looked at his watch, then at the sad rumpled bag of popcorn on Evan's desk. "Is that lunch?"

He frowned. "What? It's low-sodium."

"Oh God, that's so depressing." Casper reached into his pocket and pulled out a phone. "I'm getting us a table at Ai Fiori. Fix your tie, we're getting actual food."

AI FIORI buzzed with late lunchers, including Evan and Casper at a corner table. In Evan's life, "Italian" generally meant pasta and meat sauce, maybe some garlic bread, but he found nothing even vaguely close to that on the menu. Casper ordered for them—butternut squash soup and then spaghetti with blue crabs. Evan demurred on the wine and had water instead.

Casper ordered the house red.

"We should work out a plan for your meeting with the community board," Casper said, laying the pale pink napkin across his lap. It seemed like he coordinated with the gray-and-pink interior of the restaurant in his black pinstripe suit, pearl gray shirt, and striped tie.

Evan checked his white shirt and black suit pants for wrinkles as he mimicked the napkin move. "Or you could just go for me," Evan said, a note of pleading in his voice.

"No. You need to make an appearance, reassure these business owners that you give a shit about their vandalized alleyways and gridlock."

"Two things that have existed since the island was settled," Evan grumbled, counting pieces of silverware on the table. "They have one of the lowest crime rates in the city—I feel we should have a little gratitude."

Casper shook his head as if Evan were slightly stupid. "No one feels gratitude in this city, Evan. It's a dangerous emotion. You feel lucky, you let down your guard, and bang—someone steals your tires while you're waiting at a light."

"That is a terrible analogy. I'm definitely writing my own remarks for the meeting."

Their soup arrived. Evan poked around the puree while he and Casper made small talk about the precinct and the quiet few months they'd had since Evan took over. Things stayed simple until their entrées arrived and Evan paused the conversation to answer a text from Matt.

"He's in Baltimore until tomorrow," Evan said as he put his phone facedown on the table. "Business trip. I swear, I see him as much as the TSA at LaGuardia." The words were light, but Evan didn't mask the reality—he missed Matt, missed coming home to him. The business doing so well meant good things for his boyfriend, but it meant upheaval to their neatly organized schedule of the past few years.

Sometimes Evan let the thought creep into his mind. *It was better when he was home all the time.*

Casper seemed overwhelmingly involved with his plate for a moment, then looked up, serious in a way Evan wasn't used to seeing him.

Evan sat back a little in his chair, surprised. "What?"

"Just—nothing." Casper dug into his meal, carefully navigating the messy food and his immaculate suit.

"Doesn't seem like nothing." Evan didn't pick up his fork; he just watched Casper until the other man put his own down.

"I'm sorry. It just struck me as something I might have said about me and Tony."

"That's…." Evan started to say something, then couldn't decide how to finish the statement. *I'm sorry? That's a shame? Have you heard from him?*

*Are you implying something?*

Casper took advantage of Evan's silence, kicking back a large portion of his ruby red wine before pinning Evan to his seat with a sharp stare. "I didn't notice, you know? You have busy lives, you have careers that demand your attention on weekends. You travel because it's expected of you, and without kids at home, they're not going to ask, 'Hey, do you need to stay home this weekend because your relationship is falling apart?'"

Evan nodded, a tiny spark of relief in his chest. They had kids, he thought. Matt was utterly devoted to….

"And we swore to each other that wouldn't be us. We actually sat down and worked out a schedule, a plan for our lives, and we swore it wouldn't end like this."

Casper's voice cracked a little at the end, and Evan leaned forward, suddenly at a loss for what to do. Touch his hand? Offer a kind word?

"Casper, I'm so sorry," Evan murmured. "I can't even imagine what you're going through. Maybe—maybe you guys just need a little time to…."

"He's got a new boyfriend," Casper blurted. A few diners looked in their direction, something Casper clearly noticed.

Evan tried not to blush. "Oh, I'm…."

"Sorry. I know." Casper wiped at his eyes, turned away from the rest of the dining room. "Everyone's sorry."

"I'm sure you'll find someone else," Evan said awkwardly, cringing inside. What if someone had said that to him when he and Matt had broken up? *No use crying over a lost love! Here, have a new one!* He knew, maybe more than anyone, it wasn't that easy, even if you accepted you had more than one love of your life.

"I don't think I want to go through that again." Casper laughed, bitter and damp. He reached for his wine and finished the glass, already signaling the waiter as he swallowed it down.


EVAN AND Casper parted on the street, work forgotten as Evan encouraged Casper to go home early, get some rest. Their meal had been punctuated by Casper's quiet rants about his and Tony's careers tearing them apart, the lack of sex and intimacy, then the lack of conversation, until they were barely roommates. Oh, and wine. Casper drank a fair amount of wine.

Evan paid the bill with his American Express, cringing at the total. Then he put Casper in a cab.

Walking back to the precinct, Evan made a very conscious decision as he dodged the crowds of tourists.

The phone rang for long seconds; Evan knew Matt was probably in a meeting, probably had his phone on silent. So he wasn't surprised when his boyfriend didn't pick up.

At the tone, Evan ducked to one side against a building to block out the noise.

"Hi, it's me. I hope your meeting is going well. And your hotel is comfortable. And the plane takes off on time tomorrow, because I miss you." Evan cleared his throat, imagining Matt getting this message as he lay on the bed, tie askew and shirt unbuttoned. "In fact, call me tonight, okay? After ten?" He threw a bit of seduction—at least he hoped that was what it was—in his tone. "And make sure Jim's in his own room by then." He hung up, running a hand over his hair as he stuck the phone in his pocket.

He and Matt—they were going to make sure they were all right.


EVAN'S PHONE buzzed an hour later as he sat at his desk, reviewing loitering complaints from a building a few blocks away.

*What the hell was that? Did you invite me to call for phone sex!?*
*Maybe.*
*Oh hell yes. Ten o'clock. Make sure you're naked.*
*I said yes to the phone thing, not the sexting thing.*
*You should get out that box Griff sent you for your promotion.*
*STOP.*

*The big blue one is about my size.*
*You. Wish.*
*Maybe YOU wish.*
*I have a meeting now.*
*What are you wearing?*
*Evan?*
*Baby?*

# Chapter 5

AT HALF past midnight, Jim trekked from his garage office back into the house. Four hours ago he'd sworn to Griffin he just needed to settle a few files and then he'd be back. They'd watch a movie, go to bed early. Wink, wink, nudge, nudge.

It really was work at first.

Jim redid the camera layout for a new client's summer home. He fixed a stubborn issue with an obstructed doorway at another's office. Feeling frisky, Jim even completed the invoicing for another month.

Haight Security Unlimited kept increasing their monthly earnings at a steady clip.

And he swore—to himself—that it would be five minutes, maybe ten. Just to check his alerts for Tripp Ingersoll.

Ten minutes, maybe fifteen.

There was a quick mention in a Palm Beach society gossip column about Tripp's parents' ongoing divorce and how ugly it was proving to be. Assets needed to be divided, and lawyers were sharpening their knives for a money buffet.

What wealth of information might be hidden in those transcriptions, he thought. Much like the book Tripp wrote and the publisher killed, never to see the light of day.

Wide-awake at his desk, Jim started when his phone rang. Only one set of people would be calling him this late: the Heterosexual Power Cabal.

This time it was Ben. Jim's former roommate (and onetime crush) lived in Portland with his wife and their thriving law practice, and he handled Jim's personal legal matters, including coordinating all the other lawyers Jim had business with.

"I took a chance you'd still be up," Ben said tensely as soon as Jim picked up.

Jim didn't love that opening line; he dropped the spreadsheet in his hand, the one tracking Tripp Ingersoll's residences over the past ten years. "Everything okay? Liddy all right?" Jim asked, already clicking his link for travel arrangements.

"Sorry, that came out wrong." Ben sighed deeply. "Hi, Jim. How's it going?"

"I'll answer that after you tell me what's going on."

"It's good news, actually. I heard from the PBA lawyer an hour ago. Ingersoll's new council wants to settle."

"Oh." Jim relaxed back into his chair. "Wait, new council? Again?"

"He seems to bounce back and forth between Mommy's and Daddy's camp depending on who is paying for what. It's been a hot mess. I talk to a different paralegal every week. But the PBA is convinced this one is going to pan out."

Rubbing his left eye with his fist, Jim tried to add this piece of the puzzle. "They were trying to squeeze me for money and publicity. I'm surprised he'd give up his vendetta."

"I'm gonna guess he needs fast money."

"His parents have money."

Ben hummed through the line. "Sure they do. Doesn't mean they're still sharing it with Junior. This divorce seems to be about getting every last dollar from the other, just so they don't have it. How much time do you think they have for a grown-ass son with a black cloud over his head?"

Jim let that sink into his brain to stew.

They talked through business and then segued to Liddy and their new condo, brushing briefly upon Jim's upcoming wedding. Forty minutes later, Jim sent his love to his former roommate and disconnected the call.

It took about a second before the pleasure of Ben's company went back to being about getting Tripp.

Mom and Dad weren't paying the bills. Tracey was gone, the suit getting settled. Tripp hadn't had a job in about a year. How unstable would his life become? And what would he do if that happened? Would he snap again?

With a sense of urgency, Jim went back to his files and clippings and half-formed ideas. He needed to find the missing link, the thing that said Tripp Ingersoll was a murderer and not just misunderstood.

Jim sent out a flurry of e-mails—to old contacts in the media, to friends from college with high-ranking jobs, to retired detectives who dabbled in private investigation.

He waited for responses, refreshing every few seconds because maybe, just maybe, lips would be loosened by all the side-taking in the divorce.

Two hours later, Jim's skin pebbled with the revelations laid out for him on his laptop screen.

The first answer came from a retired Seattle reporter he'd known for two decades. Word on the street was Tracey's attempt to leave Tripp and live her life as she damn well pleased had backfired. Tripp wouldn't leave her and her new boyfriend alone, skirting the edge of stalking but never enough to get himself in trouble, so she went underground, with some help from well-off friends.

Where, Jim's reporter friend didn't know. But if he was starting somewhere, it would have to be in Los Angeles, where Tracey's trail ended.

Jim booked a ticket to LAX for the next day.


HE FOUND Griffin asleep in bed, his glasses on the end of his nose, the television blaring a rerun of *Friends*. A roil of guilt made Jim a little sick to his stomach, but God. He was just going to Los Angeles for a day or two. Talk to some people—just make sure Tracey was okay. Encourage her to go to the police, maybe.

File charges.

Help him get Tripp one way or another.

Not telling Griffin wasn't....

Wasn't....

Except that it was. Shitty.

Jim stripped down to his underwear in the bathroom. Washed up in the dark because really, his reflection wasn't anything he wanted to see at this moment. When he came back to bed, he found Griffin curled on his side, glasses on an open script on his nightstand and the light off.

Griffin was waiting for him.

Jim slipped under the covers, wrapping himself around Griffin in a desperate attempt to stave off the guilt.

"You okay?" Griffin mumbled, pushing back against Jim's body, tucking himself tighter in his arms.

"Fine," he said finally, whispering into Griffin's shoulder. "Go to sleep."

"Late...."

"I know. Sorry. Work."

Griffin wiggled around then, turning in Jim's embrace. They were nose to nose now, and Jim regretted the light on his side still being on.

"It's okay, I did it to you enough." Griffin's eyes barely opened, but the downward tug at the corners of his mouth was unmistakable.

Jim pressed a kiss there, just because he couldn't bear to see it.


"I'LL BE home in two days. I just have to make sure the house is okay," Jim said, throwing clothes in a leather duffel as Griffin watched him from the window seat of their bedroom.

"Can't the handyman handle it?"

"I just want to make sure it's okay."

Griffin walked over and put his arms around Jim's neck. His smile shook a little, but the sincerity of the words burned into Jim's heart.

"I know what Ed meant to you," he said softly. "I understand you need to handle this yourself."

Jim kissed him until he stopped talking, then took a car to the airport.


TO ASSUAGE at least a little of the guilt, Jim did drive up to Ed's house.

The handyman kept things tidy: mowed the lawn and trimmed the hedges, swept up leaves and cleared the gutters. To the naked eye, it looked lived-in.

Jim stood in the driveway, memories pushing at him like angry ghosts trying to get his attention.

Ed and Delia Kelly, heartbroken and weeping on their couch.

Bringing Ed back here after the trial ended so horrifically, after losing Delia.

Getting the news of Ed's cancer.

That knock on the door and first time he laid eyes on Griffin.

Ed's funeral.

Standing in this driveway watching Griffin melt down as he realized the depth of Daisy's betrayal.

"Oh Ed, I just want to fix this," Jim whispered before walking to the front door and letting himself in.


THEY TALKED on the phone, he and Griffin, before he went to sleep that night. (In the guest room, the one that had been Carmen's through childhood and her tumultuous teen years. It was like a little punishment for lying to his fiancé.) Chitchat, news. A reminder to call Terry and Mimi and kiss their godchildren when he stopped by.

Jim didn't miss the way Griffin's voice changed as he talked about Kelly and Jamey. Jim couldn't avoid the stories about Sadie Griffin had to share, because she was growing up so fast, Jim, and wouldn't it be great when she was old enough for sleepovers?

"I love you," Jim said, when Griffin started yawning at his end, on the other side of the country. "So much."

"What's wrong? Why won't you tell me?" Griffin asked finally.

"Just a lot of ghosts here."

Griffin made a sad sound. "Let me fly out there. You shouldn't do this alone," he whispered.

"You have things to do."

"There's something you're not telling me."

Jim exhaled. He rolled over to stare at the picture of Ed and Delia Kelly cradling their little Carmen, posed in front of the fireplace one room over. They were just a normal family, excited about the future. Thinking about more Christmases and vacations and the happy times they would have.

Tripp Ingersoll had murdered that dream.

And Jim couldn't let him get away with it.

"I love you so much, and I can't wait to marry you," Jim said finally, his voice cracking on every word. "I'll be back on Friday."

Griffin's silence was loud. And angry. And maybe a little scared. He breathed for a few moments, then sighed. "I love you too."


TWO DAYS gave Jim little time to play around. He made dinner plans with the Ohs, then drove his rental car to the airport. Los Angeles beckoned, offering the chance to dig up some dirt on that piece of shit Ingersoll.

For lunch, he drove yet another rental to a hotel in downtown Burbank. His reporter contact put him in touch with a woman who claimed to know Tracey.

Who claimed to know how to get in touch with her.

*Could it be this easy?* Jim thought as he walked through the bright lobby of the Tangerine Hotel. He checked his phone for a message. Apparently he was now meeting "Sybil" out by the hotel pool.

The strong smell of chlorine greeted him, along with a few kids splashing in the pool as three women ignored them in favor of chatting at a table with a large blue umbrella. Jim looked from one end to the other until he located a car idling on the other side of the metal fencing.

Someone waved at him from inside.

Sybil probably wasn't her name. She looked like she'd been made from the same mold as Tracey—pretty, athletic build, expensive and classic clothing and demeanor. She leaned against the door of her late-model BMW, face obscured by wide sunglasses.

She checked his ID, twice, then crossed her arms over her chest.

"So you've known Tracey for a while."

"She left him because she couldn't be sure anymore, you know?"

"Sure?"

"That he wouldn't hurt her. He always said he loved her too much to do anything like that," Sybil muttered. "She believed him for a long time and then... she didn't."

Jim let his emotions simmer, scuffing his boot against the asphalt. Behind him, the kids continued to scream with their vacation abandon, utterly overjoyed to be in a crappy pool at an airport hotel.

"So she got scared and left. Seemed like she was okay for a while. New boyfriend and everything. We told her to be out as much as possible. Because if eyes were on her, then he would have to back off, right?" Sybil huffed.

*That's also how women get killed when they leave their abusers,* Jim thought, but he nodded to keep Sybil talking.

"Then all of a sudden she freaked out. Like—on the phone, screaming and crying and saying he would kill her. We tried to calm her down, but she wouldn't listen. So we gave her some money—a lot, actually, my husband is gonna kill me." She gave a nasty little snort. "And she, uh... she went off the grid." Sybil pursed her lips and Jim got the idea that the young woman still thought her friend was being dramatic.

"Do you know how to get in touch with her?" Jim asked, his voice neutral.

"Yeah. I mean—I can get her a message."

Jim reached into his pocket, pulled out a business card. He extended it to Sybil, then took a deep breath. "Ask her to please give me a call. Tell her I want to help her. Please."

Sybil considered the card, then plucked it from his fingertips. "Okay. She'll know who you are, right?"

Jim looked over his shoulder. The kids were diving now, running down the diving board and springing headfirst into the blue water. He turned back to Sybil slowly. "Oh yeah, she'll know who I am."

*"HE DIDN'T do anything," Tracey Baldwin wept, head in her hands as they sat in the interrogation room. "He came home and he was fine! We went to bed like any other night!"*

*Jim and Terry shared a look over the sobbing girl's head. Neither one believed her account of the evening, but she remained steady, even as they tried to break her.*

*"Ms. Baldwin, what time did Mr. Ingersoll come home?" Terry asked, sliding into the seat next to her.*

*"I told you, eleven!"*

*Jim checked his notes for the hundredth time. The coroner said Carmen died somewhere between ten and twelve that night.*

*"You're sure?" Jim said sharply from across the room.*

*Tracey snapped her head up and gave him a fearful nod. "Yes! Eleven. I'm positive!"*

*They tried. Good cop and bad cop. Threats. Intimidation. None of it worked. They didn't break her that night, and not in any of the nights that followed. Tripp's alibi was solid.*

JIM DROVE back to the airport, hands shaking and eyes bleary from too much coffee and not enough sleep. Sybil might have been the start of the trail to Tripp or a dead end, someone looking to place herself in the middle of the drama. He wanted to crawl into a bed and sleep for a month, but there were still more things to check out.

Godchildren to play with.

He slept on the short flight from Los Angeles to Seattle, then took a cab to the Ohs' apartment. It was a slow trudge up to the lobby of their building—he almost fell asleep waiting for the doorman to buzz him up.

Terry greeted him at the elevator, a wide and beautiful smile across his face. "Jim!" Jim had barely stepped into the hallway before Terry tackled him for a hug.

If Jim couldn't be with Griffin at this moment, Terry made a nice platonic substitute.

"Mimi and the kids are so excited," Terry said, leading him into the apartment with an arm slung around his shoulder. "We're having pizza because Jamey insisted it was your favorite."

A shriek alerted him to his presence being detected, and from around the corner came a black-haired little boy in nothing but a Superman T-shirt, matching underwear, and a cape.

"Uncle Jim!"


DESPITE NOT producing Uncle Griffin out of his duffel bag, Jim was still an exalted guest in the Oh home. Jamey, bright and chattering, took his rightful place on Jim's lap. They shared a plate (emblazoned with a colorful dinosaur playing basketball) for their pizza, and Jamey had a Spiderman sippy cup he offered as well, but Jim demurred in favor of his beer. Little Kelly watched from her high chair, eyeing Jim with some suspicion as she ate tiny squares of pizza.

"So the movie's almost done?" Terry asked, focusing on Jim and wiping Kelly's greasy hands without skipping a beat.

"I haven't heard a release date yet, but yeah. It's in, uh, postproduction now." Jim shifted Jamey on his lap, the little boy's warmth and weight distracting him. This was how their life could be—children at a table set with plastic and hard-to-destroy silverware. Early because of bedtimes and stories and songs and baths and tantrums.

Then Jamey slid his gnawed at crusts onto Jim's side of the plate and leaned back, relaxing into Jim's body like Jim had transformed into a favorite old chair.

"There'll be a Los Angeles premiere, right?" Mimi returned to the table with a few bottles of water, her face alight with excitement.

"Yes—and I've been threatened... I mean promised that you'll all have passes." Jim smiled, curving his arm a bit tighter around Jamey.

"Oh my gosh, so exciting." Mimi clapped. "And now on to the more important date—when are you guys getting married?"

Jim poked around at the pile of bitten leftovers on his plate. Should he actually eat a slobbered-on crust just to avoid the question? "Soon. We just want this movie out and done with so we have time to concentrate."

"Of course, makes sense," Terry said. Then he looked at Jim and laughed.

"What?"

"I'm amazed he stayed awake this long. Wouldn't take a nap when he found out you were coming," said Mimi, starting to get up again. "I'll just...."

"No, I got it. My godson, my eating partner. Still, uh, the same room, right?"

Mimi and Terry shared a look as Jim stood up carefully, one hand under Jamey's butt until he could move him into a more comfortable position.

"Yeah. Second door past the bathroom." Terry gestured just to make sure.

Jim nodded, then headed across the living room to the hallway. He could hear the whispered Korean behind him and knew he'd be walking out to some questions.

Little Kelly didn't have her brother's nap avoidance problems. At nine she was still awake, chirping and drooling in all her glory as she crawled around the living room floor.

Jim couldn't take his eyes off of her.

Jamey he could handle—he talked, he said what he wanted, he could handle feeding himself and using the bathroom successfully at least 50 percent of the time. He could say he was happy or sad or angry or cold.

When Sadie was a baby—and watching Kelly now—Jim felt a fear growing in him. How could you protect them when they were that small? And if they got to the next stage, how easy was that? What terrible things could happen to Jamey, even with him being verbal? Problem was, Jim knew. Jim had talked to weeping parents and seen the tiniest body bags used for the smallest victims. He'd seen firsthand the evil that lurked in the world.

How could he possibly agree to bring children into his and Griffin's life, knowing what he knew?

"How's the new department?" Jim asked as Mimi took Kelly to get her ready for bed.

"Better. It isn't always a fun day, but you have a chance to walk away with a still breathing person more often than not." Terry had completed the classes and been moved to Crisis Intervention a year and a half after Jim retired from Homicide.

"Good." Jim slid down a little farther on the couch, exhaustion creeping in. He was glad to be sleeping on the Ohs' sofa tonight because the idea of driving and finding a hotel was just too much.

"You okay?"

Jim sighed. Behind Terry, who was reclining on the love seat, Jim could see the lights and night sky of Seattle. Sometimes he missed home—and then here he was, with his close friends, and all he could think about was the house in New York with Griffin. "Got a lot going on. Some… work with the security firm is a bit of a strain."

Terry frowned, sitting up slowly. "Wow, were you always this bad a liar?"

"I don't want to talk about it?" Jim tried.

Terry all but laughed in his face. "You have five minutes before Mimi gets back. Pick your poison—her or me?"

Jim talked quickly.


"JIM, YOU can't," Terry whispered.

"I know."

"If anyone finds out…."

"I know."

"You have to shut this down. You can't be seen as trying to track Tracey Ingersoll."

"She might be in danger."

"Don't pretend that's the reason you're trying to find her."


TERRY DIDN'T say anything after their clandestine chat. Jim lay awake on the sofa, staring at the white ceiling and the shadows playing across it from the lights outside. On his phone waited ten messages and pictures from Griffin, who'd decided to paint the den while Jim was away. He looked at the shot of Griffin, smiling and mussed with green paint on his nose, mugging for the camera, for an hour before his phone battery started to die.

# Chapter 6

GRIFFIN STOOD in the dining room, taking deep, calming breaths. Everything looked and smelled perfect: table set with fine linens and cut crystal, candles, and pale roses, china that rarely saw the light of day from his dad's house. Jim was coming home from his trip, and they were going to celebrate.

They were going to talk.

His heart raced a little as he walked into the kitchen. Georgia, bless her heart, had outdone her culinary self with a three-course meal of Jim's favorite foods from their Hawaii stay. Two courses of pork and a chocolate cake—basically, Jim Nirvana. There was no doubt what this was—a bribe, a peace offering, a moment to butter Jim up before they laid it on the line.

Griffin had one question to ask, and it was the one that everyone told him was crazy. The one question Daisy and Evan and his father heard and patted his hand, shaking their heads with smiles on their lips.

"He loves you so much. He doesn't regret getting engaged."

They had logical reasons, all of them. Soothed his fears and petted away his anxiety—until he left lunch or their house or the coffee shop on Main Street and it all came rushing back.

In a perfect world, Griffin got Jim and a wedding ring and two kids and happily ever after. That was the dream. But in the end, the truth was, he'd take Jim and call it a day. A good day.

A perfect day.

JIM KEPT his voice low as he talked on the phone. The driver from the car service seemed wholly uninterested in the conversation, but Jim's healthy sense of paranoia had skated over to something a little more serious.

"Thank you for calling me," he murmured.

Tracey Baldwin Ingersoll sniffled on the other end of the line. "I'm not sure this is a good idea."

"I want to help you," Jim cajoled. "Just talk—see if there's something I can do so you're not so scared."

She didn't say anything for a few minutes. Jim's heartbeat ratcheted up.

"You're trying to put him in jail. Still," she said finally.

Jim counted in his head, kept his breathing steady. "Yes. I am," he said, taking a chance with honesty. "But that's secondary to you feeling safe and able to live your life."

Another pause, another pregnant moment of tension that burned Jim's throat and chest. "Okay. I'll... I'll meet you."

He didn't pump his fist or react other than closing his eyes. Oh God. So close. "You pick the place and time. Anything you want."

"I'll call you back in a few days," she said softly. "I just need to figure out a safe place."

"Of course. Call me anytime," Jim said soothingly. "Anytime."

She ended the call without saying another word.

Jim stared out the window as the New York state countryside whooshed by, and tried to breathe through the rapid beat of his heart.


DODGING OUT of the shower, Griffin rummaged through his dresser until he found an older white button-down—relegated to "knock around" status due to its less than crisp look but soft to the touch and with the laid-back sexy he was going for. A pair of khakis completed the outfit, and barefoot, Griffin hurried downstairs.

The car service said five, and it was quarter 'til.

He ran back to the kitchen, double-checked the food warming in the oven. Beer, chilled glasses, enough ice if they decided to do after-dinner drinks. Whipped cream for sexual purposes because Jim hated it on cake.

Loved it on Griffin.

"Maybe I should put a tarp down in the living room," he muttered, walking quickly back to the dining room.

Then the living room. Fire in the fireplace, extra blankets laid on the ottoman, lube and condoms very much out in the open on the coffee table.

This was no subtle seduction.

STARING WITHOUT really looking, it took Jim a few minutes to realize they were nearly to the house. He shook his head slowly, sifting the Tripp thoughts back into the locked box and bringing the love of his life to the forefront. Home, Griffin, real life, business with Matt, weekends up at the Drake house in Albany or movies or retiling the guest bathroom. This was life he loved, the one he was protecting.

Jim slipped the phone out of his pocket and sent off a quick text to Matt.

*Back. Don't bother me until Monday.*

A few minutes went by, but his phone buzzed.

*You old dog. Don't throw your back out.*

And then a winky face a few seconds later.

The driver pulled the car up to the mailbox just past the front walkway. Jim saw Griffin through the giant picture window, watched him pace back and forth for a second before realizing the car was there.

Griffin waved, then darted out of sight.

Jim had the car door open before Griffin could do the same to the house.

"Hi!" Griffin called from the open doorway, framed like an ad for something wholesome and sexy and inviting. It would say, *How could you not stay here forever and love this person, because he's one of a kind.*

The driver opened the trunk and Jim forgot he was the kind of guy who carried his own bag because all he could focus on was getting to the front door.

"Best thing I've seen in a while," he said with a grin.

Griffin rolled his eyes, but Jim could see how much the compliment pleased him. "You better not be talking about the shrubs," he teased.

Jim walked the last three feet and met him on the top steps, unable to stop smiling. "I can literally only see one thing right now," he whispered, caught in Griffin's gaze. "And that's you."

"Oh God, that's so cheesy," Griffin laughed, but he wound his arms around Jim's neck, and the solidness of him—the sheer pleasure of feeling like he was home in that second—made Jim shiver.

"Hi," he whispered, brushing his mouth against the skin he could reach at Griffin's open collar.

"Hi." Griffin made a little sound of pleasure but shifted away just enough to avoid Jim's mouth. "Sorry," he said over his shoulder.

That was when Jim remembered the driver.

"Tip him a lot of money so he leaves faster," Griffin whispered in his ear. Jim smirked as they untangled, and then he turned around.

"Thanks," Jim said, friendly, like the bored-looking man hadn't just watched a cheesy commercial happen on the porch. He handed him a twenty, which didn't evoke a reaction either.

Jim grabbed his duffel, then watched as the guy pivoted away to trudge back to the car.

"He seems nice," Griffin said and then pulled Jim into the house.

THE DOOR slammed behind them and Griffin didn't say another word— he just grabbed Jim by the shirtfront and pulled their bodies close, slotting them together with the muscle memory of two people who'd loved only each other so long it was DNA-deep habit.

"I have dinner ready, I have new sheets on the bed, and there are condoms on the coffee table—you tell me what you want first, baby," he murmured, locked in to Jim's everything.

Jim blinked in surprise. Then his face bloomed into a smile that went straight to Griffin's cock. He wrapped his arms around Griffin, slotted his thigh between his legs, and ground their bodies together.

"Fucking, food, then fucking," he whispered, enunciating each word and letting the last one linger.

Griffin's entire body flared with heat. "You gonna make it upstairs?" he asked, innocent in tone but wickedly punctuated by his hands sliding under Jim's windbreaker and down to grab his ass. "Or...."

Jim didn't answer. He was already freeing one hand to pull at Griffin's khakis, tugging them down over his hips. Griffin laughed in response, pulling at Jim's jacket.

Griffin pulled away as they started to get tangled in mutual want and stubborn clothing. He kept his gaze locked on Jim as he reached for the buttons of his shirt.

"I get a show too?" Jim asked, his voice cracking as he pulled off his own jacket and let it fall to the floor.

Mouth watering, Griffin nodded. He let the white shirt slide down his body and pool at his feet. Then he undid the buttons on his pants as he walked backward toward the staircase separating the foyer from the living room.

"You get whatever you want," Griffin whispered as his pants slid down his legs. He kicked them aside, then leaned back against the banister.

"YOU ARE the sexiest thing I've ever seen," Jim said, sliding out of his shoes and unbuckling his belt with one hand before he stalked toward Griffin. Naked Griffin, in just his glasses and a smile that Jim wanted to capture in a bottle and have forever. "Sit down."

"My ass is going to get cold." Griffin pouted, but he moved and sat down slowly on the bottom step.

Jim would have taken pity on him, but then Griffin leaned back, opening his legs slowly, ever the wicked tease. "I'll make sure to warm it up later," Jim teased, kicking off his jeans.

"Is that a spanking reference, because no—until you convince me otherwise."

Snickering, Jim dropped to his knees, barely even feeling the hard floor underneath him. This wasn't going to be a long-term thing, but right now he felt far too frisky to adjourn elsewhere. He pressed his hands against Griffin's chest, hair tickling his palms as he stroked downward to his thighs; it felt like he was mapping his fiancé out, remembering every hard curve of muscle and how they fit together.

Griffin blinked lazily behind his glasses. "Good news—my ass is warming up," Griffin said, matter-of-fact as he took his own cock in hand, a slow stroke from top to bottom that made Jim's mouth water. "If you feel like swapping tonight, I might be interested. Maybe if you're nice I'll let you do it twice."

"Maybe I'll tie you to the bed and do it whenever I feel like it," Jim countered. The delighted expression on Griffin's face was painfully arousing.

"Is that what you want?" Another stroke and Griffin bit his lip, moving his hips restlessly.

"Yeah, right after you fuck me," Jim whispered, standing over Griffin's beautiful body, just as desperate as his love.

Griffin stopped touching himself, licking lips as he leaned forward. "Fuck, you're pretty," he whispered, laying his hands on Jim's hips. He just needed to move a bit more, open his mouth and take Jim down his throat, but he didn't. The moment of anticipation built until Jim could see they were both shaking with it.

Jim slid his hands into Griffin's hair before straddling his lap. He dropped down, already grinding as their bodies touched for the first time in far too long. They wrapped around each other, Jim hungry for Griffin's mouth and his lover scrabbling his hands over Jim's skin.

It was always good, but this was... anxiety and guilt and love so deep it hurt Jim to taste Griffin's mouth.

THEY MADE out in a furious tangle of hands and legs and mouth until Griffin said "ow" one too many times. Jim stood up and pulled him into the living room; Griffin tripped over discarded clothes and Jim's bag, barely made it to the open space in front of the fire. He went down hard on his ass but didn't have time to complain because Jim was already on top of him, frantically rubbing their cocks together.

Maybe he would come this way, just to take the edge off, but any hopes of completion went out the window when Jim backed off and started kissing down Griffin's body. Griffin pulled his glasses off, pushed them to safety under the recliner, then held on for dear life.

Jim reached his cock and bit the insides of Griffin's thighs until Griffin kicked—because no, no teasing, he hated it unless it was the kind where he loved it and Jim held him down by the hips. But then Jim decided it was enough—time to lick his cock in long, slow strokes, moaning as he tasted Griffin with absolute abandon. He moved his fingers under Griffin's knees and calves, spreading him out to trail kisses lower and never in one place long enough.

Griffin tried to breathe.

"Fuck, I missed you so much, I miss you all the time," Jim whispered, pulling back from each bite and kiss to blow on the sting. Then he moved again, before Griffin could respond, to take him deep inside his mouth.

Griffin couldn't stop moving, couldn't stop pushing up into Jim's mouth, couldn't stop the relentless need pulsing in his body. It was almost enough—so close—but Jim pulled away again, sitting straight up to leave Griffin panting and moaning on the floor.

"What...," Griffin panted, but Jim was moving—he grabbed the condoms off the table, threw one at Griffin, then went back for the lube.

Shaking, Griffin tore open the package. Everything was blurry, but he could hear the sounds coming from Jim, and he knew what they meant.

Intimately.

"Ugh, no, let me help," Griffin whined, sliding the condom on—finally, God—and sitting up as he grabbed frantically for Jim.

"I got it," Jim said, laughing a little, but Griffin didn't stop being handsy as hell.

"I love it, I love your body, God." Griffin knew he was talking nonsense, knew there wasn't much sexy about a guy with a condom on his dick in the middle of the living room, but he just didn't want to stop touching Jim at this moment. Or any moment, ever.

"I got it," Jim said again, pushing him down on his back, then climbing over him.

Griffin moaned when he realized what Jim was doing. "Oh God, is it Christmas?"

"That's so...." Jim's breath caught, and Griffin bit his lip in hopes the pain would stop him moving—or coming—as Jim shifted Griffin into position. With one hand, he held Griffin down, pushing against his chest. With the other, he guided Griffin inside, slowly, with heavy breaths.

Eyes fluttering closed, Griffin ground his teeth through the familiar and exquisite pleasure of sliding into Jim.

Griffin grabbed Jim's hips, pressing his fingers into his skin. He braced his feet against the hardwood floor, gritting his teeth as Jim slid the last few inches and came to a rest seated in Griffin's lap.

There was a pause, Jim shifting and breathing until he was comfortable, Griffin rigid and sighing underneath him, forcing his eyes open so he could look up at Jim.

"Fuck, I love you so much," Jim murmured, so perfect in the firelight that Griffin felt a little dizzy. He knew what was coming next, knew the way Jim's body moved up and then back down with slow intent.

SOMEWHERE IN the moment, a tiny brush of guilt reared its ugly head. Jim clenched, squeezed on Griffin's dick as he held it deep inside, then raised his hips—locked down on the pressure he knew he would feel—and began a punishing pace of riding up, pushing down, choking on the pleasure/pain of the intense burn. He closed his eyes because looking down at Griffin would be his undoing.

Faster and harder, sweat rolling from his skin, Jim slid his grip to rest against Griffin's neck, cupping it in his hands as he moved his lower body in a frantic rhythm. "Come on," he panted. "Come on."

"Jim, slow down," Griffin choked out, but Jim didn't even break the wild need to finish—for Griffin to finish, for Jim to feel grounded in his lover's arms.

There was no finesse to his movements, just an animalistic sense of urgent need, a violent push toward completion.

THE VISELIKE clasp of Jim's body on his dick, the pressure, the longing he'd felt for so long—Griffin couldn't hold back much longer. He grabbed Jim's wrists, holding on for dear life, sweat dripping off their bodies as Griffin slid against the rug.

"Please," he panted, imploring with his pleas and scrabbling hands. "Please, please—love you."

"Show me," Jim answered, pressing his forehead to Griffin's, breathing hard into his mouth. "Come inside me."

All Griffin could do in response was open his mouth in a silent cry, arching his body against Jim's. The orgasm racked his body for long shuddering moments before he collapsed against the rug.

His eyes closed as Jim kept moving, kissing Griffin's face with frantic damp movements of his lips. "Love you," he kept saying, rocking over Griffin, trying to find his own completion.

Griffin reached between them, closing his hand over Jim's cock, the way eased by sweat and Griffin's fervent need to tip Jim over the edge.

Jim lasted a few more seconds, but Griffin knew how to pull an orgasm from this man—knew how to twist and tug and bite his shoulder, how to rock up his hips and read that perfect moment when Jim lost it.

Wildly, roughly, completely.

They lay there, wet and shaking on the rug, like they had run a marathon.

And won.

"Hell of a homecoming," Jim whispered into Griffin's ear. He'd tried to move, but Griffin held him in place despite the fact that he was heavy and lax and probably hurting.

No. Griffin wouldn't let him go.

"I missed you."

"It was two days."

Griffin nudged him and shifted until they were looking each other in the eye. "It's been longer than that."

Jim swallowed. "Yeah."

EVENTUALLY THEY showered—together. They dressed in clean pajamas, threw everything discarded on the floor downstairs down the laundry chute, and ate a romantic meal for two by candlelight in the dining room.

He pushed their chairs closer together and they held hands because Griffin refused to let Jim get farther than a foot away and Jim couldn't deny him.

"I, uh, got a new project," Griffin said eventually.

Jim girded himself for the news—the schedule in Los Angeles, the continuation of a schedule that made them both unhappy. "Oh. Okay. Where are you filming?" he asked, neutral.

"It's a play. We're going to do it here in New York."

Looking up, Jim met Griffin's pleased expression with one of his own. "Wow."

"Yeah, it's something Shane wrote a few years ago that they never produced. Bennett said I could pick anything, and that was the one I liked the most." Griffin's excitement began to pick up. He squeezed Jim's hand and gestured with the other. "These two friends pretend to be dating so their possessive exes will leave them alone. It's sort of a comedy of manners but with a bit of melancholy underneath, because of course one of the men has always had a thing for his friend. Eventually the man goes back to his ex, and the other one decides they can't be friends anymore. Shane is going to do some rewrites and...." Griffin's voice peaked into shy delight. "I'm going to produce it."

Jim pushed his chair back just in time for Griffin to slide into his arms. "Baby, that's great. Congratulations." And it was great. Because Griffin would be on the East Coast with Jim—the small voice reminding him about Tracey and Tripp and the whole fucking mess be damned—and they would get married.

It would be fine.

"It's a little scary, but I mean, I can have a home base, you know? I'll work in the city when we start staging, but the rest of the time I'll be home. Mostly." Griffin scooted even closer so he could put his arms around Jim's shoulders, his face morphing from happy to nervous in rapid succession. "That's okay, right? That I'm here all the time?"

"What the hell kind of question is that? Our first date was a week long—I'm completely used to you being underfoot."

"Jackass."

IN BED a few hours later, Griffin lay in Jim's arms, the little spoon to Jim's big one. It was dark and quiet, and Griffin had run out of time. He wouldn't be a chicken. He would just say—

"Do you want kids?"

Jim's voice rang out so suddenly that Griffin almost rolled off the bed in shock. He caught his breath, then attempted to roll over, but Jim kept him pinned, his back to Jim's chest. "What?"

"The way you are with Sadie—I'm not blind. I know you want to have kids."

Griffin began to shake because... oh God. He needed to ask his question, but right now it was buried under an avalanche of other things, other elephants sitting quiet watch in the room. "I...." Griffin gulped in air, courage. "I do. I mean, I love Sadie. I love our godchildren, but sometimes I think—I think I'd like them to be mine."

The silence rested over them then, Griffin's heart beating so wildly he felt dizzy. Jim's arms tight around him kept him grounded and held him prisoner at once.

Griffin felt trapped in the moment, in the dark, so he took a breath, said a little prayer to his mother, and whispered, "Are you sure you want to get married?"

He inhaled, lungs burning until Jim kissed the back of his neck tenderly. "So sure I want to marry you."

"Okay." Griffin pinched himself, just to make sure this was real.

"We should set a date."

"Jim, that's not why I asked," Griffin murmured.

"I know." Jim rubbed Griffin's chest gently, rolling over until Griffin was almost on his stomach. Another moment that felt like before, when they were fucking, like Jim was protecting him. "I want to set a date because I love you. Because it wasn't a big elaborate proposal—I just opened my mouth and boom, there it was. You make me want things I never imagined I could...."

Griffin felt his throat closing up with emotion. Jim's weight pushed him into the mattress, his soft words squeezing his heart.

"I want to marry you and I want...." Jim breathed deeply, then blew out a stream of warm air against the back of Griffin's neck. "I want to talk about the future. Who we see—sharing our home."

"Oh God." Griffin laughed, searching for a joke before he burst into tears. "I've been so scared to talk to you about this. I know your aversion to dirt and drool."

Jim shrugged, big and warm around Griffin's body. "Will I traumatize a kid if I'm wearing plastic gloves?"

"All the time?"

"Most of the time."

"I think Matt knows a shrink—we should talk to her first."

They joked back and forth for a while, voices growing softer. Griffin felt himself drifting off even as Jim kept talking about buying stock in a paper towel company and swapping out the rugs for hospital-grade linoleum until Griffin fell asleep, content and overjoyed.

# Chapter 7

EVAN HADN'T bought a new suit in a few years and certainly not for a date. But right now he walked into Gotham Bar and Grill with Matt's hand at his back, wearing a three-hundred-dollar suit and a shiny pair of wing tips.

It was a little overwhelming.

After three weeks of missing each other—and an inordinate amount of phone sex—Evan and Matt had made a very specific plan for the night. Danny and Elizabeth were with their aunt Elena for the weekend, leaving the two men with an empty house. Matt had put Jim in charge of the business phone as a repayment for that "Weekend of Humping" he had previously covered, and Evan had said a quiet prayer that the status quo would prevail in his precinct.

They were alone and focusing on each other.

At the moment, however, Evan paid attention to the classy, filled-to-capacity restaurant, and followed the hostess to their table. Buzzing with energy, Matt pulled out his chair and Evan sat with a tiny smile.

Across from him dropped Matt, looking fit and tan as ever, in a swank black suit and dark blue shirt. The collar was open—and then an extra button that seemed to take the look from "attractive" to "distracting." Evan did his traditional glance around their surroundings, but even that didn't stop him from sliding his hand across the table.

Matt's eyes flashed with surprise, but the smile that crossed his lips as he took Evan's hand in his was one of absolute delight.

Distracting, times ten.

"To what do I owe this honor?" Matt said softly, leaning forward as he stroked his thumb over Evan's wrist.

Evan shrugged. "I like that shirt," he responded casually, delighting at the sparkle that flickered across Matt's face.

"How much?"

Evan leaned forward, avoiding the candle and flowers between them, avoiding the tables on either side with their chatting diners. "I hope you don't have any plans to get out of bed until Sunday," he murmured.

Matt licked his lips.

Evan smirked.

The waiter, who'd probably been standing there for a few minutes, cleared his throat.

GOTHAM'S FOOD was amazing, which made letting go of each other's hands all that much easier when presented with a rack of lamb to die for. Ankles locked under the table, Evan and Matt ate, split a bottle of wine, and shared smug smiles. It felt like a spell wove around them, locking out anything that might upset the moment.

"I want to bottle whatever has gotten into you tonight," Matt said, wiping his mouth with his napkin. "And then I want to mass produce it."

"Stop sounding so surprised. I'm capable of—things." Evan squinted at him over the table. Mr. Lightweight and three glasses of wine—the evening promised to get even more interesting.

Matt snickered. "You called them things."

"That's all they're getting called in public." Evan rubbed his ankle against Matt's, and that simple act did marvelous things to everything below Matt's belt.

"Prude," Matt teased, reaching across the table to take Evan's hand in his again.

"I'll remember you called me that tonight." When Evan ran his tongue over his lower lip, Matt nearly fell off his chair.

"I've created a monster."

MATT TRIED his damnedest to get Evan into the men's room with him, but even slightly tipsy, his boyfriend put the kibosh on that.

"Public lewdness? Really?" Evan hissed as they walked out onto the sidewalk. "Absolutely not."

So Matt grabbed his ass while hailing a cab. It seemed a good compromise.

Inside the cab, Evan dropped his head against the seat back and Matt had to surreptitiously adjust himself as they zoomed uptown to their next destination. No public lewdness, but how did Evan feel about a blow job in the back of his cab?

"No," Evan said, and for a second, Matt thought he had spoken out loud.

"Did I say—"

"I know you," Evan laughed, rolling his head to one side and regarding Matt with fond irritation. "So no."

"No?" Matt pouted, then dropped his hand to Evan's knee.

"Matt."

"Mmmm" was his only response. He tested each inch on the inside of Evan's thigh, hitching up bit by bit until the fabric bunched and pulled as Evan moved his hips against the creaky faux leather seats.

"Matt." Different tone this time, softer and pleading. Matt bit his lip as he laid his head on Evan's shoulder, dancing his fingers up to Evan's belt.

"Gonna take you home and rip this gorgeous suit off your body," Matt whispered, laying his palm flat against Evan's stomach, feeling the trembling, marveling in the moment. "Gonna open you up with my mouth and fuck you all night." It was a calculated risk—Evan might get mad at him crossing a line—but when he went limp instead of rigid, Matt purred.

And then he bit his tongue to keep from moaning when Evan pushed Matt's hand between his legs.


EVAN STUMBLED out of the cab at Eighty-Fifth Street, right in front of the venue of the GOAL fundraiser. Tipsy and so turned on, Evan straightened up, then turned to watch Matt join him on the sidewalk.

After he adjusted himself, of course. The expression of irritated pain included flared nostrils and pursed lips.

"Oh my God," Evan said before hiccupping into laughter. No more wine. Ever.

"You're a cheap, easy date," Matt huffed. He put an arm around Evan's waist. "And I seriously fucking love that."

Evan pulled himself together, attempting to get his suit to fit, because right now it wasn't. It was practically falling off—in his mind, at least—as Matt led him through the elaborate lobby and past the evening-shift security.

"Hopefully they know it's an LGBT event," Matt said dryly, "so it's not a surprise you look like a rent boy."

"I do not!"

Inside the mirrored elevator, Evan got a good look at himself—flushed, rumpled, and still not quite "calm" in his pants. He fumbled with his tie and then his jacket, not noticing until too late that Matt was pressing up against his back.

"Stop that." Evan tried to be stern—tried hard.

Hard.

But Matt was gorgeous and he put his arms around Evan's waist and God. That spot at the back of his neck that Matt kissed so gently.

At some point Evan was going to sober up and be horrified by his unexpected behavior. Right now? It just felt good to sink back in Matt's arms. All his nerve endings were sparking at the same time, keeping rhythm with his heartbeat.

"This night was an excellent idea," Evan murmured, watching the picture they made in the mirror.


MATT THOUGHT about pushing his luck. The restaurant, the cab ride, this moment—it wasn't Evan's usual MO, and maybe Matt could convince him to find a closet, but no, that metaphor didn't play right in Matt's head.

He pulled away and gently put Evan back together, their gazes never breaking in the mirror.

By the time the elevator dinged open, Evan looked slightly less discombobulated and Matt felt like an actual grown-up.

Hand in hand, they walked into the space. High soaring ceilings and Italian architecture greeted them, along with the quiet murmur of the crowd. A small band played jazz standards in the corner.

Three hundred or so supporters of the Gay Officers Action League mingled under dimmed lights, sipping cocktails and writing checks.

Matt generally liked the GOAL crowd. No one gave him shit about his own difficult dealings with the NYPD, and at least a few of the younger officers thought he was some sort of folk hero.

That was nice, he wasn't going to lie.

And the fact that Evan had joined the group first, that Evan served on a committee—that Evan was holding his hand as they walked into the ballroom...

Well, he loved this fucking group like crazy right now.

"Drink?" Matt asked as they navigated the tables, looking around to see where to start. A long row of prizes sat sparkling and inviting under the lights, with folks putting their raffle tickets into huge champagne glasses next to each.

"No. Let's just get some tickets. I'm feeling lucky tonight," Evan said, keeping Matt close as they reversed course.

Matt laughed delightedly. "Me too."

They chatted as they moved along the prize table, hip to hip, dropping tickets here and there. Matt put a handful of little red squares in the glass for a trip for two to Paris, waggling his eyebrows at Evan.

Evan shrugged. "I'm sure if you asked Bennett, he'd send you."

"Sure. But the point is you and I going to Paris. Alone. Without working."

Evan's expression got subdued for a second, and the smile that followed didn't seem to help the chill that fell over the evening.


"WHAT'S WRONG?" Matt finally asked. Evan had a club soda and Matt a beer; they'd found two empty seats at a back table, right next to an expanse of high windows that provided a view of the river and the bridge. He moved his chair closer to Evan's side so their bodies touched; Evan's stiff posture softened a little, and he looked up, his expression serious.

"You're okay with our lives, right?" Evan asked finally, breaking the pregnant pause between them with six words.

Matt shook his head as if to clear his previous assumptions about what Evan had to say. Being too sexual in public, he'd thought. Maybe. Evan's boundaries had relaxed over time, but before—that was wild for them.

He wasn't expecting a wider spotlight.

"Of course I am." Matt leaned into Evan's space, grabbing his hand. "Of course. Where the hell is this coming from?"

Evan started to shake his head, opened his mouth as if to say something, but the moment shattered as Matt heard someone calling for Evan.

Casper Vaughn, in a slick black tux, was walking across the floor toward their table.

Evan brightened as Casper got closer, and Matt found himself irritated by the smile on his boyfriend's lips. Weren't they just having a serious conversation? Why did the appearance of Casper Vaughn grind everything to a halt?

Standing, Evan extended his hand, and Matt watched a friendly handshake turn into a half hug.

He stood up so fast his chair almost tipped over.

"Matt, you remember Casper, right?" Evan said, stepping back so Matt could offer his hand, presumably.

Matt put his hands in his pocket, just because yes, he was that much of a dick.

"Matt, of course." Casper pulled out a chair and sat down without an invitation, and Matt decided he was also a dick and rude to boot. "Wow, what a night."

"Everything looks great. I bet you're relieved it's over." Evan sat down as well, and Matt finally followed suit—after pushing his chair so close to Evan's he was pretty sure there would be damage to the wood.

"Casper's the chair of the committee," Evan said to Matt, and Matt pretended to care.

"Yes. Been working on this pretty much nonstop." Casper made a hand gesture, then shrugged. "Not like I have anywhere else to be."

Evan made his sympathetic face. "You should try going out once in a while," he said. "I know they have some bar crawl thing—Jesse mentioned it at the last meeting."

"That's not really my scene. Twentysomethings in skinny jeans drinking microbrews—no, thank you," Casper said dryly. "I'm looking for something a little different."

"You don't have to do anything," Evan laughed. "Just—go out."

Matt watched their conversation like a Ping-Pong game, then realized Casper was without a very specific accessory: his boyfriend.

Then the exchange made sense.

Sense that Matt didn't like at all.


CASPER STUCK around longer than Evan expected, but he understood. Everyone here was still looking over Casper's shoulder for Tony, and every single glance was a reminder of something lost. He got it—got it too well. So he didn't mind when Casper shadowed them from the table to the bar and then went with them to stand by the pillars to listen to the winners of the raffle being read.

Matt sulking—and throwing down beer after beer—Evan chalked up to their night of hedonistic behavior being temporarily halted so he could cheer up a sad friend.

Evan fully intended to cheer Matt up once they got home.

"THANK YOU," Casper said as they stood on the sidewalk. It was midnight, and the rest of the party milled about, saying their own good-byes and hailing cabs. Matt nodded at Chris Callas and her wife, then Jesse and his husband, who didn't notice as they made out from the front door to the waiting taxi.

Kids. Lucky them.

A "bar in a basket" nestled in his arms, Matt waited for Casper to finish his sad-sack sighs and disappear. Evan was nodding, touching his arm. Matt wanted to throw the vodka bottle he'd won at Casper (what the hell kind of name was that anyway?), then grab his boyfriend and escape back to Brooklyn.

Another hug and Matt felt his blood pressure notch up. Casper gave him a half smile, like he had just remembered Matt was standing there, before heading to the cab line forming along the sidewalk.

"Oh hey bye," Matt called to Casper's back.

Evan moved to stand directly in front of him so he couldn't see anyone else. "Hi."

"Well, that sucked."

"You won vodka," Evan said, patting the cellophane monstrosity. "Most of our friends are drunks, so that will be put to good use."

"You're chipper." Matt made it sound like it wasn't a good thing.

"I sobered up and we're going home to an empty house—why wouldn't I be chipper?" Evan took a breath and leaned in for a kiss. A very public kiss, with tongues and everything. Matt opened his mouth to deepen it, letting Evan's tentative push become something very, very dirty.

When Evan pulled back, he had a ridiculously proud grin on his face. "Let's go home."

THEY WERE in bed an hour later, everything discarded for "tomorrow" as they fell onto the mattress in a heap. Evan kept trying to move, but Matt wasn't having any of it. It still felt surprising when they were like this, like Evan the Alpha Male just dropped and rolled over like... like every terrible slur he'd heard in the almost fifty years of his life.

But even with the rough hands and filthy litany pouring from Matt's mouth, nothing felt as safe as Evan holding on to the sheets for leverage as Matt pounded their bodies together.

# Chapter 8

"SO AUGUST 1," Matt said, carrying the box of cameras into the elevator of Bennett's building. He and Jim were there for the next-to-last phase of the security build-out—the offices of a rich guy who made movies and bankrolled plays was more secure than the fucking White House.

"August 1." Jim leaned against the elevator wall, carrying a tray of coffee and all their blueprints, neatly housed in a portfolio. "You got plans?"

Matt smirked. "I'll clear my schedule."

"How do you feel about taking on a job?"

"You need security for a wedding?" Matt said teasingly. He knew what Jim was going to ask, but it didn't hurt to make him work for it.

"My God, you're an asshole." Jim got a little pink as he shifted from foot to foot. "Wanna be a best man?"

"I feel like I'm already—"

"Okay, I'm done. I'm asking anyone else in the world but you."

Matt threw his head back and cackled.

"Seriously."

The elevator opened and they got out, jostling each other's shoulders.

Their crew was spread out, already working. Matt dropped the box of cameras at their central workstation, some empty cubicles that would eventually house interns in the fall.

Jim handed out coffees to the two supervisors of the crew, Eddie and a new freelancer named Alex.

"It's like a broad shoulder parade in here," Matt said as he walked up to join the trio. "We should be lifting heavy things instead of installing tiny cameras."

Eddie smirked. "You sure about that? At your age—"

"Shut up." Matt and Eddie had had a running thing about age since the day Eddie realized he was born the same year Matt graduated high school.

"Concerned about your brittle bones, there, boss," Eddie said, all innocent as he picked up the blueprints on the desk. "You need a nap or anything, you just press your panic button—"

Matt flipped him the bird and everyone laughed.

Jim and Matt went up to the second floor, where they'd already installed the security system.

"Well."

"Well what?" Jim was flicking through his phone, not looking up.

"Ask me again, properly, please," Matt said sternly.

Jim cleared his throat before glancing up. "Matt, you incredible asshole. Will you be my best man?"

Matt rubbed at his eyes, sniffling dramatically. "Yes, Jim. Yes."

Jim kicked him. Hard.

On the second floor, the receptionist, Hilary, greeted them politely.

"Bennett in?" Matt asked.

"He's, um—he's got someone in there right now. Mr. Lowry."

"Oh, well that's fine." Matt started down the hallway with Jim behind him. "He's a friend of ours."

They got halfway there when Bennett's door opened and hit the wall with force. Matt stopped, surprised at the vehemence of the slam.

Shane stepped out of the office, red-faced and angry in a way that Matt had literally never seen. Lighthearted and charming, Shane always had a smile on his face, was always the guy breaking up bad moods and bad moments, the perpetual clown.

"This is fucking ridiculous," Shane spat as if no one was in the hallway. "You should be ashamed of yourself."

He turned, saw Matt and Jim, and visibly put himself back together. Or at least tried.

"Hey, guys, sorry," Shane muttered, then pushed past them as he strode down the hallway and out the door.

No one said anything; Matt felt frozen to the spot, trying to decide whether to follow Shane to make sure he was all right.

Bennett stepped into the hallway, white-faced and clearly enraged. "What?"

Matt rocked back on his heels, trying to find his way through a completely unfamiliar conversation with a man he considered to be his friend. "Is everything all right?"

Bennett waved his hand, gripping the doorway with the other. Sweat dripped down his face, a scowl planted there. "It's none of your damn business. Go finish the installation," he snapped, cold and rude.

"Excuse me?" Matt's hackles went up. This wasn't their relationship—business never got in the way of their friendship, and Bennett had never acted like an asshole before. This wasn't the way Bennett talked to him. Ever.

"I said go finish the fucking installation. That's what I pay you for."

"Hey," Jim started to say, but Bennett tore back into the office, then pulled the door closed with such force that something on the interior wall tipped over and crashed.

Part of Matt wanted to kick open the door and tear Bennett a new one. No one talked to him like that. Ever. Especially not someone he considered a friend. Whatever fight he and Shane had, Matt wasn't involved.

"What the fuck was that?" Jim asked behind him, just as bewildered, judging by his tone.

"I have no idea." Matt turned around to find a wide-eyed Hilary and Amy, Bennett's assistant, standing at the end of the hallway looking shocked.

This wasn't Bennett's normal behavior with *anyone*.

"We should...."

Jim held up his hand. He already had his phone to his ear.


THEY WENT back downstairs to check on the work. Eddie had everything in hand; it was more an excuse to duck into an empty office to talk.

"Griffin said he hadn't heard anything from Daisy, nothing the matter as far as he knew. They just had breakfast this morning," Jim said, sitting on a desk and shaking his head. "She seemed fine."

"Evan said he talked to Helena briefly—nothing to add." Matt paced the small office, kicking bits of plaster littering the floor on each pass.

Jim shrugged. "So he's probably having a shitty day and he's taking it out on everyone. You saw Shane."

"Yeah. I saw Shane. You ever seen Shane without a smile on his face?" Matt did another turn. "He looked pissed. He's never pissed. I didn't think he had that setting."

"They'll figure it out. Bennett will apologize. Probably buy you a boat to show how sorry he is," Jim said dryly. He dropped his empty coffee cup in a tiny garbage can, currently empty despite the construction crap all over the room. "Let's finish this job. I have things to do back at the house."

"Yeah, yeah." Matt ran both hands over his hair and kicked his final piece of ceiling. "Let's get out of here."

An eyebrow raise from Jim at the utterly unprofessional idea coming out of Matt's mouth. "I thought…."

"Eddie can handle it. We're gonna go get lunch, charge Bennett's corporate account, and then head home early. I gotta start working on my best man toast."

Jim laughed as he stood up. "You're only allowed to say 'fuck' twice and you can't mention we had sex that one time."

Matt pulled a pout. "Well, there goes my reading during the ceremony."


"I DON'T like this guy sniffing around Evan," Matt said as Jim was about to put a dumpling into his mouth.

It dropped off his fork and back onto his plate. "Excuse me?"

"This guy—PR douche bag. We know him from the gay cop organization, and he's just—I don't know. He and his boyfriend split and all of a sudden it's 'oh hey me and Casper had lunch' and 'oh Casper's texting me,'" Matt bitched, stabbing at his egg roll with a knife.

Because he valued his life, Jim didn't laugh.

He wanted to. But he didn't.

"You think Evan might…."

Matt rolled his eyes. "No, I don't think Evan would even notice some guy trying to get into his pants. That's not the point."

"So the point is no one should find your boyfriend attractive?"

"I mean—this guy has nerve, to be putting the moves on someone clearly in a committed relationship," Matt said with a huff.

"But Evan won't do anything."

"No."

"So your issue is someone thinks your boyfriend is attractive."

Matt scowled. "Shut up."

"He doesn't have any exes for you to be jealous of," Jim said delicately. "At least no one to worry about coming back into your lives. So this is new for you."

Matt threw his napkin at Jim's head. "I have a shrink for shit like that. As my friend, you're supposed to agree this guy is a douche bag and offer to hit him for me."

Jim turned a laugh into a cough. "Right. Okay—that."

"You are no help. Literally."

"Matt, you can't say any of this to Evan." Jim speared the dumpling again and enjoyed the moist combination of lamb and cabbage as Matt stewed across the table.

"Why not?"

"Because your closest male friend is someone you've slept with," Jim said gently. Quietly. "And Evan behaved badly toward me, which hurt your feelings."

Matt's face twisted into something angry and resigned. "He's never slept with the douche bag."

"And he won't." Jim poured them both more tea. "You know that, I know that. The only person who might not understand that is this guy—"

"Casper."

"Casper? Jesus, that's a douche name."

"I know!"

"Casper might sniff around Evan, and he might be less than a real friend, but that isn't your business. My future husband is best friends forever with someone who once almost ruined his career. I can't say anything. We share a life, but that's... she's his. I'm part of your life. Evan—Evan tolerates me."

"He likes you," Matt argued.

"Now."

Leaning back in his chair, Matt nodded. "Now."

"Now he trusts me. Now he's okay with us being friends and working together every day. He trusts you. You have to give him the same courtesy."

Matt blew out a dramatic breath, then leaned back over the table. "Fine. I hate you for being rational."

"If you tell Griffin this story, he'll come up with an elaborate plan to put Nair in the guy's shampoo bottle, like he's James Bond at summer camp," Jim pointed out as he forked another dumpling. "So that can be your backup plan."

# Chapter 9

THE TABLE was set for four—reset after dinner for two. Elizabeth and Danny ate plates of pasta at six, with Matt and Evan hanging around the dining room to chat about the day. A rare lazy Saturday turning into a Sunday—maybe a movie, maybe the park for a bike ride. It was quietly domestic, and Evan felt himself relaxing for the first time in two weeks.

After Bennett's weird blowup, Matt's mood had been dicey to say the least. Instead of giving the apology everyone expected, Bennett went behind closed doors on a daily basis, and Matt refused to make the first move. The whole thing snowballed into Matt turning the office remodel over to Eddie and Alex entirely, choosing to work at his house or Jim's most of the time.

No one could get more information than that. Helena hadn't even known there'd been a fight when Evan talked to her, but that was also because of some serious stress in her career.

To the surprise of no one, Helena was tendering her resignation to the NYPD. She missed working with Evan, didn't like his replacement, and found the new captain rigid and uncompromising—not to mention harboring an ancient attitude about women and the police force. She was miserable and done. Now it was just a matter of choosing something else.

She and Evan talked for almost three hours. He tried to counsel his dearest friend, but he didn't have answers for her. Particularly when she confessed Shane was having some career pains himself and he'd suggested they move to the West Coast for a while.

That played in Evan's head as they cleared the table after the twins were done and had disappeared upstairs for the night.

"Helena said she and Shane were considering a move to California," Evan said suddenly as they walked into the kitchen. In front of him, Matt paused, then turned, a frown on his face.

"What?"

"When we talked. She's going to resign, Shane's talking about California. I don't know—it just seemed to come out of nowhere."

They loaded the dishwasher in silence. Evan was lost in thought, but Matt looked concerned.

"What?"

"I don't know. What if something is going on with Bennett? Like money problems or something? He spends like he's fucking Midas."

"I think he spends like that because he can. And even if he was in trouble, I have to imagine there's some sort of backup plan." Evan assumed. Evan *hoped*. Because Bennett wasn't just Matt's client, he was their friend. And the aftershocks of Bennett's business tanking would spread through their social circle in a serious way.

Matt wiped his hands on a dish towel, leaned against the counter. "It's not because he's our biggest client," Matt said. "We've got plenty of business and we're fine—we'd be fine."

Evan nodded. Things would change, but everyone was still going to get through college, even if they had to take out loans.

"Just—I keep thinking about last summer and all of us at the house. Everyone so damn happy."

The note of defeat in Matt's voice moved Evan around the open dishwasher and into Matt's embrace. They hugged until the oven timer went off. Evan dropped a kiss on his boyfriend's cheek before he walked away.

They'd been through bad times—times they wouldn't wish on anyone else. The specter of darkness wasn't welcome in the lives of the people they loved.


"SO SHANE and I just have to finish a few things; then we'll move to the next stage of development," Griffin said, taking a break between courses to give an update on what he was doing. The two couples sat around the dining room table, enjoying a meal Matt had made himself—though Evan took credit for the salad.

And pouring the wine.

Evan and Matt shared a look that Griffin couldn't help but notice.

"How's Shane been lately?" Matt asked, leaning on the table on his elbows. He'd been about half as jovial as usual, which Griffin found concerning. The question about Shane ratcheted it up another few notches.

"Uh, fine. We've been mostly working via Google Docs and stuff like that. This bathroom renovation is basically never going to end, and with Jim going out of town so much for work, someone's gotta make sure no one is tracking molecules of dirt through the house." He patted Jim's hand affectionately. "His HEPA filter only does so much."

When no one laughed, Griffin scrunched up his face in concern. "What?"

Another shared look. Then Evan updated them on his conversation with Helena—by the end of which Griffin was moving into low-level panic.

"Shane wants to leave? That's crazy," Griffin said. "And Bennett hasn't apologized." The panic inflated a tick more. "Daisy said...." He paused, torn between his worry and the fact that she had said things in confidence.

"Daisy said what?" Matt asked.

It was the concern in Matt's voice that loosened Griffin's tongue—because he knew Matt felt protective about his friend, and maybe what he knew was bigger than bitching about your husband. "She said that Bennett's been working all the time. Like getting in late, taking a lot of meetings during the day. He's always out doing something, apparently."

Again, Matt's expression did something to Griffin. Something upsetting.

"What? Is that not true?"

"He's in his office all the time," Matt said, reaching for his wineglass. "Never goes out. That's what Alex told me. They can't even get him to inspect the second floor so we can officially sign off the job."

Jim took Griffin's hand and squeezed, and all the while Griffin felt the blood draining from his face. "Someone has to tell her," he started to say, but Evan was shaking his head.

"You can't put yourself in the middle of this, Griffin. Tempting as it is. It's their marriage."

"She's been through this shit once before," Griffin snapped. "And now there's a kid involved."

Evan smiled sadly. "She knows something's wrong already—if you're going to say anything to her, it should be that she needs to talk to her husband."

The conversation killed the mood for a while until Jim let out a loud sigh and started refilling wineglasses. "Time for a change in conversation. Someone ask Griffin about how many tiny squares of material are sitting on our dining room table."

Pulled out of his funk enough to be annoyed, Griffin kicked Jim under the table. "We have to pick curtains for the bathroom and linens for the wedding."

"I told you. Black."

Griffin looked at their hosts but realized he was getting nothing from Matt and Evan. Their house was nice, but everything was a shade of brown or rust.

Worst gays ever.

"Black is bad luck at a wedding."

"What about tuxes? They're black," Matt put in, and Evan started laughing. "Everyone has black tuxes. So black is not bad luck, unless you consider getting married to be unlucky—"

"Black linens are for goth raves and over-the-hill birthday parties," Griffin cut him off in midsentence. "If I let Jim plan the wedding, it would be a barbecue with beer balls and a sheet cake, and the wedding favor would be Wet-Naps."

"I love everything about that sentence," Matt said.

Jim gestured toward his friend. "See!"


GRIFFIN HELPED Evan with the dishes as Jim and Matt caught the end of the baseball game on television.

"I feel like gender roles are being—" Griffin started, but Evan put up a hand. There was cheering from the living room.

"What?" he yelled.

"Grand slam!" Matt yelled back.

Evan looked pleased as he went back to putting silverware in the basket. "Sorry, what were you saying?"

Griffin started to laugh, shaking his head as he pointed to the living room. "Go. I can finish this."


DESPITE THE serious conversation at dinner, the rest of the evening was nice. Evan liked spending time with Jim and Griffin, liked their banter and obvious affection for each other. Where once he'd been so awkward with that sort of exchange—and if he was honest, that predated Matt—now it made him feel warm inside.

"You didn't tell me Jim asked you to be his best man," Evan said, stripping back the blankets on the bed. The air conditioner hummed as the water from the bathroom indicated Matt hadn't heard him. Evan waited a second, then tried again, louder.

"Heard you the first time," Matt said, poking his head out of the bathroom door. "Yeah, it was the same day as the Bennett thing, so I guess I forgot." He shot Evan a big smile. "But yeah—tux and speech and all that other shit."

He looked pleased, and Evan returned his smile. "That was nice of him."

"Well, he's probably the best guy friend I have," Matt said with a shrug, disappearing back into the bathroom. "Besides you."

"I'm your friend?"

"You started that way," Matt said, coming back out of the bathroom again. "So yeah."

"Oh." Evan got into bed and leaned against the headboard.

Matt snapped off the bathroom light, then walked around the bed to his side. "'Oh' is a weird response." Matt slid under the covers.

"Not really. I'm just sort of ranking friends in my head." Evan laughed at his own words. "When I was—with me and Sherri, she had her friends, I had work people. Vic and Helena. Then I had you. Now I guess I'm trying to figure out who my friends are."

"Well, there's Casper of course," Matt said, the sharpness of his tone pulling Evan out of his musing.

"I guess. Casper's more a work friend."

"Does he know that?"

Evan looked down at Matt's form, facing away from him. "Of course he does."

"Uh-huh." Matt punched his pillows and maneuvered himself around until he was comfortable—behavior Evan knew usually meant *leave me alone.*

He slid down under the covers, then reached over to shut off the light.

# Chapter 10

WHEN TRACEY didn't call back, Jim took it as a sign.

He hid the Ingersoll file further in the computer, away from his line of sight. He worked on the security business; he oversaw the final bathroom remodel as Griffin spent a week of long days in the city with Shane, working on their play.

Every day, another piece of the wedding planning seemed to show up in the dining room. Jim grumbled and blustered about the clutter, but then Griffin would smile as he walked into the room and Jim couldn't get pissy about it. Not really.

Not when it made the person he loved so happy.

When his cell rang with an unknown number as they walked the aisles of a local furniture store, Jim didn't think about it, he just hit Accept.

"Detective Shea? It's me, Tracey."

JIM LEFT Griffin to look at mirrors, whispering about a work call. He hurried away from the other shoppers and his fiancé, who looked annoyed at the intrusion on their Sunday afternoon.

He all but ran out to the parking lot so he could pace on the grass median.

"Yes, Tracey. Sorry, I'm here," he whispered, out of breath.

"Can you come up to Toronto? On Wednesday. This coming Wednesday. I'll be there and I'll talk to you."

Jim's heart nearly beat out of his chest. "Yes, absolutely. Where can I meet you?"

They agreed on nine in the evening, at the Trump International Hotel. She'd text him her room number that day. No one could come with him; no one could know about their meeting.

"I understand," Jim said, watching the entrance to the furniture store, waiting for Griffin to come out, for him to demand Jim tell him what was going on. He felt like a felon sneaking around to hide his secret life. "I'll be there."

Tracey disconnected the call and Jim sat down on his haunches, shaking in the warm spring afternoon air.

GRIFFIN LET the annoyance fall by the wayside. He had to be patient with Jim's work, just like Jim was patient with him. So maybe he was considering using Jim's obvious guilt to get his way for the color scheme of the wedding. And the purchase of a new mirror for the upstairs hallway.

None of this was bad stuff.

And maybe, just maybe, he lingered in the aisle with the baby furniture, pretending he was looking for a present for Sadie when really he was filling the second guest room like the nursery he dreamed it could be.

Jim found him there but said nothing as they walked to find a salesman.

At lunch Jim was his attentive self, holding Griffin's hand and patiently listening to updates about the project. Shane, Griffin gossiped, refused to say anything about Bennett, insisting it was personal and not work related. He didn't want to talk about leaving New York at all.

It was weird.

Jim nodded and commented in the right spots; he even asked about Daisy and Sadie and the latest adventures of their weekly excursion.

Griffin did twenty minutes on the lemurs at the zoo and Jim didn't yawn once.

If it was strange and out of character, Griffin just tried not to look a gift horse in the mouth.

THE TRIP to Toronto made him worry. A little bit.

JIM SWORE he would just listen to Tracey, see what she had to say, but he couldn't sleep in the days leading up to his trip. He found himself spending more and more time with the files, with his research, searching for a pattern or a clue. Something he'd missed. Because if he had this time with Tracey, he needed to ask the right questions or it would all be for nothing.

Putting pressure on his relationship for nothing at all.

The day before he left to meet Tracey, Jim found himself on a forum for retired detectives. There was a shit ton of bitching about pensions and waxing poetic about "the good ol' days," so Jim was in full skim mode.

Until he found the section on unsolved cases.

This was what he needed for validation: more ex-cops like him still tangling with a piece of human garbage they wished they'd put away. Maybe he wanted reassurance he wasn't crazy.

It was a detective from a small town on the California-Oregon border called Ashland that caught his eye. Ashland, home of Southern Oregon University.

Jim blinked. Why did that sound so familiar?

Because Tracey Baldwin went there, he realized a second later, and then the rabbit hole opened up and swallowed him.

The first murder was a coed found in a bar parking lot a few miles away from campus. The detective on the case noted another girl under similar circumstances in a university town about fifty miles away.

He knew it in his bones, in the marrow that made him a good detective—he knew he'd found it, and all hell broke loose.

Jim started pulling up names and pictures and newspaper accounts. Six hours later, as dawn peeked in through the blinds, Jim had five murders in five cities, an almost straight line from Northern California to Seattle. A spree that started in Tracey Baldwin Ingersoll's college town and ended in Jim's backyard.

His hands shook slightly as he dove into Tripp Ingersoll's college years. He had everything publicly available, from newspaper clippings to four yearbooks, hidden in the back of a filing cabinet.

Nothing matched up.

Jim pushed away the frustration and stared at the five dead girls on his desktop.

He thought about Tracey.

Then he found her yearbook.


TRACEY BALDWIN, women's lacrosse, four years.

Their team's schedule the year of the murders.

He sat back in his chair and breathed through the heart attack he was sure he was having. How did he miss this the first time around?

Right. Jim and Terry were hell-bent on getting Tripp for Carmen Kelly's murder. They had tunnel vision.

Now?

Now Jim had a pattern of murders, strangulations like Carmen's, matching the travel of Tracey Baldwin's lacrosse career during college. If he could prove that Tripp was with her...

If he could get these cold cases reopened...

If.


MATT DROVE him to the airport. The atmosphere was so tense, the air so thick, that Jim kept the window rolled down just so he could breathe.

"I'm going to take everything you have and lay it out," Matt said as he pulled into the departures lane for LaGuardia Airport. "Time line, case files."

"We need his schedule," Jim murmured, rubbing damp hands on his pants. "His class schedule, attendance if we can get it."

"I'll get it." Matt eased to the curb and put the SUV in park. He glanced over at Jim, who nodded.

"Thank you."

"Remember what Liz said about talking to Tracey."

A phone consultation with Matt's dear friend Liz the shrink had produced an outline of information for talking to an abused woman. Whether or not Tripp ever used his fists, he'd most definitely used fear to keep Tracey in line—for who knew how long. Jim's handling of Tracey's trauma might be the difference between getting what he needed and leaving empty handed.

Start slow and easy.

Ask open-ended questions.

Let her tell the story in her own way.

Explore her options for getting her life back.

Most of all? Jim had to stay calm.

"You go, you talk to her, we give everything to the police in the first town where that girl died." Matt's jaw was tense as he laid out their agreement. Again. "Then this is done."

Jim put his hand on the door handle. "We have to give them as much evidence as we can," he argued quietly. "This has to stick."

"You have no jurisdiction and this guy is fucking suing you. If this gets out, that lawsuit might not go away any time soon."

Jim opened the door, grabbed his bag in his other hand. "It's not going to get out." He stepped out, then closed the door behind him. Jim leaned against the window, fully owning up to the anger on Matt's face. "It's not. Don't worry."

Matt didn't look convinced, and as Jim walked into the terminal, he felt his friend's eyes boring into the back of his head.

# Chapter 11

"ARE YOU sure about this?"

Griffin stood in the foyer of his house, clutching Sadie against his chest. The toddler was currently trying to strip off his glasses, so he was dodging her like a prizefighter. She found this game hilarious.

"It's a few days. She'll be fine," Griffin said soothingly. "You need this—you both do."

Daisy looked like hell, a condition that Griffin couldn't sit idly by for. Whatever rough spots in their past, Daisy was his friend, his sister, his family—and if he had to be a busybody to help her, so fucking what.

Which was exactly what he was going to say when everyone got on his case about it.

"I don't know what's wrong. He's acting so weird," Daisy said, rubbing her eyes. Nothing about this picture gave him any comfort. Daisy looked like hell in jeans and a T-shirt he suspected was Bennett's. She'd driven up by herself with Sadie in the backseat—almost unheard-of behavior given Bennett's overprotectiveness. The overnight bag she had carried in—well, Griffin was fighting to keep a calm face.

"And you are going to deal with it, whatever it is," Griffin said softly. He let Sadie win the game and have his glasses; it gave him a chance to walk over to Daisy and pull her against his free side.

"Momma," Sadie said, petting her head.

"Yes, Momma needs to go talk to Daddy, and we're going to have so much fun," Griffin said brightly, even as he felt Daisy's tears against his shirt. "Can you say 'bye, Momma! Love you!'"

Sadie didn't quite get the game, but she smothered Daisy's face with kisses and waved at her a few minutes later as Daisy pulled herself together at the open door.

"I love you," Griffin said, and Daisy gave him her best brave smile. "Bennett loves you—remember that."

"I know." Daisy blew kisses to Sadie, who was now wearing Griffin's glasses, and then she was gone.

Griffin looked at the—blurry—closed door, then at Sadie, who was blinking at him behind his round glasses.

"Oh Sadie girl, what are we going to do with these people?"

JIM STOOD in the posh lobby of the Trump Hotel, hands in the pocket of his suit pants. A small overnight bag sat next to the sleek tan leather chair he'd claimed. He'd spent two hours of coffee and texting with Matt, going over the specific dates and times they needed Tracey to confirm.

He had to get something from her, something that would compel the Ashland detectives to act.

And now it was going to happen.

Tracey had sent him a message from another unknown cell number, and in a few minutes, they would meet.

It didn't take long to spot her. She walked out of the elevators a few feet from where he was waiting, dressed in a smart black pantsuit, her hair tucked up in a simple twist.

Jim blinked. Liz had him prepared for a broken woman, a woman overwhelmed by her fear as she hid from her husband.

Tracey looked like a model.

Her smile was meek, though, as she spotted him. They met in the middle of the elaborate gold-and-mirror lobby. He extended his hand like this was a casual meet-up with an acquaintance.

"Detective," she murmured, her hand cold and small in his.

"You can call me Jim."

THEY SETTLED into the seat grouping farthest away from the check-in desk. Tracey's back was ramrod straight, hands folded in her lap. Jim settled across from the couch. He smiled tightly, trying to remain calm and focused on the young woman before him.

"I appreciate this, Tracey. I want you to know, before we start, that if you need assistance—if I can help put you in touch with people."

Tracey nodded, twisting a slim gold bracelet on her wrist. "Thank you. I'm all right for now. My parents have been helping me with some money and uh—once the lawsuit is done…." She trailed off as Jim shifted in his seat.

Money for the divorce, Jim assumed. He didn't bother to comment.

Silence settled between them as the murmur of guests arriving and departing around them swarmed.

He cleared his throat and began.

"I don't want to talk about that girl in Los Angeles," Tracey said softly. "You can't do anything to him because—"

"I know," Jim cut in, rubbing his hands on his suit pants. Calm, he reminded himself. Calm. "We don't have to go over that." The urge to ask her about providing his alibi hurt as he buried it down deep. "Can we talk about you and Tripp in college?"

Tracey's doe eyes widened a fraction. "College?"

"You went to Ashland, in Southern Oregon."

She nodded slowly.

"And you played lacrosse."

She tipped her head to one side as if trying to figure out his line of questioning. "Yes. Four years."

From memory, Jim reeled off some of the colleges she had competed against, mixing up various schools with the towns where the murders occurred.

She nodded through each one. "That sounds right," she said as he finished his list.

Jim's heartbeat sped up. He could feel his mouth drying up, his tongue swelling as he pressed it against the roof of his mouth. "Did Tripp ever travel with you?"

"My sophomore year," Tracey murmured, a tiny hint of a smile playing at the corners of her mouth. "He said he would miss me too much if he didn't."

It was all Jim could do not to get up and beat his chest.


HE VIBRATED from the Trump Hotel to the airport to the plane. He texted Matt everything Tracey told him, hands shaking as he settled into his first-class seat.

They had confirmation.

Jim reined in his emotions as best he could, but the replay loop in his mind would not stop.

Before they parted, Tracey had shaken his hand, her voice soft and tremulous. "He told me I'd end up like Carmen if I didn't watch myself. That's why I left, you know. That's why I'm getting the divorce. His parents are going to have to give me what I'm owed."

The only thing Jim could focus on when she said that was the confession woven through Tripp's threat.

He might not be able to put Tripp away for Carmen Kelly's murder, but he knew, even if no one else ever would.

"I'm going to get him, Ed. It's almost done," he whispered before shooting off a text to Griffin.

*I love you.*


GRIFFIN HANDLED a bout of tears when Sadie realized that the "bye, Momma" game ended with Momma being bye-bye. They sat on the living room floor and played with the box of toys Griffin kept for her; Sadie found a purple stuffed monkey that she immediately began cooing to and petting like it was a baby doll.

"Okay, purple monkey baby makes you happy, which makes me happy," Griffin murmured, stroking Sadie's fine dark hair. His phone buzzed, which caught her attention. Griffin pulled Sadie into his lap so he could read his message.

"See? Uncle Jim loves Uncle Griffin," he said, showing her the screen.

Sadie made the purple monkey kiss the phone, and Griffin's heart melted.

*I have a surprise for you!*

He hoped said surprise would push his fiancé a little further down that long hallway toward fatherhood.


JIM FELT amazing. Jim was jazzed and pumped and ready to come home and suck his fiancé's brains out through his dick.

Twice.

So when he tipped the driver before heading to the front door, there was a spring in his step. Then the door opened and, well....

"Uncle Jim's home! Hi, Uncle Jim! Sadie's having a sleepover!" Griffin enthused.

Sadie waved a purple monkey at him.

He got three kisses after that—one slobbery, one stuffed, and one from Griffin that included a brightly desperate smile.

"Don't kill me?"

THEY ATE pizza in the living room, Jim remarkably calm about a child, red sauce, and crumbs coming in contact with a rug and the upholstery.

"We've had sex on this rug—she can drop a crumb," Griffin muttered.

"I'm fine. I didn't even say anything."

Sadie ignored them both. She sat primly with her back against the recliner, a dish towel tied around her neck and a large plastic plate in her lap. The monkey sat next to her, similarly decked out. Griffin cut her slice into smaller pieces, and she ate each one carefully.

The monkey was not hungry.

"You know, I actually think she's cleaner than you," Jim observed, reaching for another slice from the box on the coffee table. "Think I can make a trade?"

"Haaaa. You're a laugh riot." Griffin offered her a juice box. She leaned over and took a sip, then went back to her pizza.

When he looked up, Jim was staring at them. Him.

"What?"

Jim smiled then, one of those smiles that had a terrible effect on Griffin's knees. Lucky he was sitting on the floor. "Nothing."

BATH TIME started well, but that ended abruptly when Sadie tried to take the stuffed animal into the tub. Griffin couldn't get her to stop crying, so Jim plucked the monkey from her hands, then proceeded to give it a "special bath" in the sink with a washcloth and Griffin's toothbrush for behind his ears.

Sadie sniffled a few times, then consented to getting washed, but only if Uncle Jim brushed the monkey's fur.

Jim was glad Griffin didn't have a camera.

Sitting on a closed toilet, brushing a monkey with one of Griffin's seven hundred hair accessories. Watching Griffin handle Sadie like a pro—from hair to ears to crevices where pizza crumbs had gotten into, he kept her laughing and content the entire time.

*He's going to be such a good father*, Jim thought. His hands tightened around the monkey as Griffin wrapped Sadie in a giant towel. Her shrieks of laughter as Griffin pretended to lose her in the folds made Jim smile.

"Pajamas and stories!" Griffin yelled as he scooped Sadie into his arms.

Jim followed as if pulled by an invisible string.

GRIFFIN FELL into bed, utterly spent and deeply happy.

Jim was home, Sadie had gone to sleep, and no news from Daisy felt like a good thing. Clearly she and Bennett were taking advantage of baby-free time. Everything was good and right in his world.

"So, you're good at that," Jim said, lying down next to Griffin. They hadn't even washed up or changed into sleep clothes.

Griffin turned his head to Jim and smiled. "I told you. Several hundred nieces and nephews. Not my first rodeo."

"Now see, I know that in theory, but this is the first time I saw you...." Jim rolled closer, pressed a kiss against Griffin's cheek.

"I love taking care of her, Jim," Griffin whispered. He tucked his forehead against Jim's neck, letting the contact bolster him. "And I feel like—my career is settled, we have a home now, a real home, we're getting married."

Jim twined their hands together.

"Have you thought more about it?"

"Yeah," Jim said quietly. "I have."

The silence that followed was killing Griffin, literally sucking his life away. But before he could open his mouth, Jim made everything perfect.

"Let's have a baby."

MUCH LIKE when he had proposed, all of Jim's carefully planned and thought-out life decisions went out the window. Spending the evening with Griffin playing godfather and caregiver tugged at Jim's emotions. Maybe it would be all right—Griffin would clearly be the hands-on parent. And Jim would be there, strong and steady, supporting his Griffin.

No. God. No, wait.

Jim put his arms around Griffin, who was babbling in utter delight at Jim's words.

He wasn't going to be his father. He'd figure this out, how to be a good dad. How to be like Ed Kelly, who loved his girls so much he had suffered just for the privilege of having them in his life.

He could....

The doorbell rang, shattering the moment.


IT DIDN'T ring once. It kept ringing.

Griffin ran down the stairs, calling for Jim to check on Sadie to make sure she hadn't woken up. He slid across the foyer, then pulled open the door, not even looking to see who was on the other side.

Daisy, hysterical and sobbing, fell into his arms.

# Chapter 12

MATT WAS halfway through his morning cup of coffee when his cell went off. The kitchen bustled with activity—Evan getting his breakfast, the twins in and out of the refrigerator.

"Yeah, hey, Jim," Matt said, taking his coffee and his phone into the living room. "You on your way? You have to be at the offices by nine."

"Sorry, Matt—you're going to have to take this one." Jim sounded exhausted, and Matt's first thoughts were: more of the Tripp Ingersoll case. He ducked out of the kitchen and walked into the farthest corner of the living room for some privacy.

"We had an agreement about this fucking—"

Jim cut him off. "Daisy showed up here at about midnight," Jim said coolly. "She left Bennett."

Matt stopped short. "What?"

"Apparently he fucked an old boyfriend a few weeks ago. Claims it was a one-time thing, but Daisy wasn't having any of his bullshit." Jim was whispering now, and Matt heard a door open and close. "She drove up here and fuck—I haven't slept, Griffin hasn't slept. It's a mess."

On the one hand it made sense, given Bennett's behavior, but Matt couldn't reconcile this man, so protective and loving and devoted to his wife and daughter, cheating. Anger started to boil up inside him. "Fuck," he swore.

Footsteps behind him made him turn; Evan stood there, looking confused.

Matt held up a finger, then went back to Jim. "So you can't come down here today?"

"I'm a hazard on the road, and frankly someone has to be around to mind the kid because Griffin's got his hands full with Daisy."

Matt blew out a breath. "Okay, I'll figure something out."

"I'm sorry."

"No, it's nothing you can help. Give Daisy my love, okay?"

"Yeah. I'll call you later."

Matt switched off the call and threw his phone across the room onto the couch.

"What's wrong?"

Sighing, Matt turned back around to Evan. "Daisy left Bennett. Apparently there was someone else."

Evan looked about the same way Matt felt—shocked and a little sick. "Jesus. I'd never expect him to be the type...."

Matt shrugged. "No one expected this. And now Jim can't make it to the inspection today or the afternoon meeting. Shit." He was supposed to work from home today and Jim was handling the appointments in the city. The kids both had things after school. "I need to go into the city."

"You can't."

The words stopped Matt cold. "What?"

"Danny has a game and Elizabeth's got dance at five." Evan looked at his watch. "I'm late."

"You're late? For a community meeting on parking meters or something?" Matt snapped.

Evan narrowed his eyes. "You need to take care of this. I can't."

They didn't fight. It wasn't their thing. There was grousing and maybe some passive-aggressive door slamming, but they didn't do this.

But Matt was standing in the middle of the living room watching Evan put on his suit jacket, and he thought his head might explode. "You're the fucking captain—you can leave a few hours early once in a while," Matt said sharply. "And please don't act like I'm making this shit up. You and I both know—"

"We both know that I'm being scrutinized more than most, and we both know that your job is flexible. Mine is not." Evan grabbed his keys off the table near the door, and Matt felt the vein in his head throbbing.

"You're just going to leave—"

"I'm sorry, but I'm late."

Incredulous, Matt watched as Evan opened the door and left.

*Left.*

"What the almighty fuck." Matt exhaled. When he turned around, Danny and Elizabeth were watching wide-eyed from the kitchen.

MATT CALLED the phone tree, parents who came through in emergencies when Matt was out of town.

No one was free—apologies all around—and Matt got angrier and angrier with each call. Why was this his problem?

*Oh right, because you made it your problem*, Matt thought. He sat in the parking lot of the high school, angrily pressing buttons.

He tried keeping up a smile for the kids, but no one believed him, so he wiped the fakery off his face, gave them each ten bucks, and waited for them to laugh at the old joke.

Nothing.

The last person he called was the one person he feared might say no just to spite him. "Miranda?"

"SO JUST pick them up, get them where they need to be, and feed 'em?" Miranda asked.

Matt rubbed his forehead. "Yeah, I'm sorry—will you be okay leaving work early?"

"I can take the afternoon off. Don't worry about it." Miranda called to someone in her office; then Matt heard a door close. "What time will you be home?"

"Six or seven."

"Dad still rolling in around nine?" It was a joke except for the part where it wasn't.

Matt didn't laugh. "Yeah. Or ten. He usually calls."

"Right. Food, or am I doing the No Dad, Let's Have Takeout Thing?"

"There's food in the house. Make two vegetables."

"Cool. Do you mind if Kent comes over?"

"No, that's fine. No making out on the couch, though," he teased, letting himself unhitch from the anger for the time being. He owed the girl big, particularly considering their truce was still written in wet ink.

Miranda snickered. "No promises."

A nice moment. Matt would press this into his scrapbook right after "Fought with Evan."

"Just—thanks, okay? I appreciate this."

Miranda's response was so blasé, he knew it wasn't a shot or a pointed remark. "You forget, Matt, I used to have to do this for Mom all the time." Noise started up again on her end, and she told someone to hang on. "I gotta go. See you tonight."

Matt didn't say good-bye, he just sat in the parking lot for a while, stewing over her words.

MATT SHOWED up at Bennett's office after nearly a month away.

His mood registered somewhere between "fuck you" and "fuck you twice"—and the fight with Evan and what Miranda said sat in his stomach like a festering wound.

Goddammit.

On Bennett's floor, everyone was walking around with white faces and zipped lips, hands tightly clutched around files and tablets and coffee cups. Matt got a few nods and a plaintive look from Amy.

He knocked on Bennett's office door loudly, then stood back to wait.

The man who answered the door bore very little resemblance to the put-together millionaire Matt had known for the past few years. Red-rimmed eyes, unshaven, his clothes dirty and askew.

Matt felt a twinge of sympathy, but that dissolved into anger at what Bennett had done to Daisy. "We have the final walk-through today for your security system, Mr. Ames," Matt said coldly. "Let's get started."

Bennett leaned against the doorjamb and started to cry.

THEY SAT on the couch in his office, Bennett with a bottle of water he wasn't drinking and Matt with a coffee. No one said anything for a while until Bennett wiped his eyes with one shaking hand.

"Are they all right?" he croaked.

"They're fine," Matt said shortly.

"With Griffin and Jim?"

"I don't think it's appropriate for me to say."

Bennett seemed to sink a little bit lower. "Please make sure—I'll give you whatever you want, just make sure they're safe."

"Don't worry about Daisy—she's my friend. I don't need any money to make sure she's okay."

"I'm sorry for how I behaved toward you—" Bennett began, but Matt put up a hand to stop him.

"I have a contract to finish and then I'm done."

Bennett sighed, leaning back into the leather sofa. "I thought we were friends."

"Me too."

They walked through the second floor; Bennett clearly wasn't listening to a word Matt was saying, but Amy and Hilary were taking notes, so he kept going. Was it one of the young men in the office? He found himself checking everyone who walked by for their reaction, for Bennett's. Something awful and uncomfortable rose in Matt's chest. He knew they were wrong and ugly to think, but his old fears were never fully exorcised from his system. What if Evan met a woman, decided to go back to something more familiar?

"If you have any questions, just call the office," Matt said in conclusion, directly addressing the two women standing to his left. "You have all the codes?"

Hilary nodded. "Yes, thank you, Matt."

They all shook hands while ignoring Bennett, who'd wandered over to look out the window. Matt stared at his back, roiling with irritation.

And then he got mad at himself for walking over.

They stood shoulder to shoulder, watching Bryant Park pull lunch-carrying worker bees and curious tourists to its green canopy. Matt tried to sort through the puzzle pieces of his annoyance and worry as Bennett breathed wetly next to him.

"I don't know what happened," Bennett whispered. "I don't—I haven't seen him in ten years, and then he came back and I thought… what if I made a mistake?"

Matt curled his hands into fists. "A mistake? You thought your relationship was a mistake? Then you know what? Tell your wife you're confused before you fuck someone else," he said, low and cold.

Bennett bowed his head. "I can't explain it," he whispered. "I… panicked. He was someone I was with for a long time…."

"You *were* with him. Past tense," Matt snapped. "Now you have a wife and a kid. All that sun and moon and stars bullshit—doting on her, making her feel like she could trust you." Matt's heart beat furiously in his chest. He wanted to take a swing at Bennett's head, knock some sense into him. "How many other people did you fuck behind her back?"

"There was no one else," Bennett insisted, shaking his head. "No one—just her."

"If that were true, she would be waiting for you at home."

Matt couldn't take another second of his presence, so he turned away without another word and left.

# Chapter 13

EVAN SPENT the entire day feeling like a massive asshole.

Yes, he had meetings to attend. Yes, he had things to do. But in the end, he couldn't bypass the fact that all of it, every irritating piece of paper that crossed his desk, every phone call that involved him being helpful and not effective—all of it could have done without him for a few hours.

He replayed the fight with Matt a thousand times, each version tightening the vise on his stomach a bit tighter. The worse part was, how many times had he had that fight with Sherri?

The indecision of what to do next haunted him. Call Matt? Text him? Leave early and take care of the kids? By then it would be too late. Matt would have already rearranged his schedule.

Jesus, he was a dick.

"Stop thinking so hard, you're going to hurt yourself."

Evan looked up to find Casper in his doorway.

"Come on, it can't be that bad."

"Yeah, actually, it can."

THEY SPLIT a bag of Swedish Fish from the vending machine, and two sodas. Casper took off his jacket and Evan shut the door, because for five minutes, he was going to vent his spleen and maybe figure out what the hell to do next.

"So you just left?" Casper asked, his voice even.

"Yes. I left him to deal with the day and never even called to make sure it was taken care of." Evan flicked one of the limp red fish across his blotter. "Which makes me an incredible asshole."

"Or a guy who's trying to get out of a shitty precinct and prove that a gay captain isn't a liability or a publicity stunt," Casper responded.

Evan looked up, surprised. "I thought you of all people would agree with my asshole assessment."

"Why? Because my relationship broke up?" Casper leaned back in his chair, a tired smile on his face. "It wasn't our careers that broke us up, Evan. It wasn't even taking each other for granted. It was about wanting different things." He shrugged one shoulder, casual and dismissive. "One day you realize that all those plans you made weren't feasible anymore. Or necessary. Right now he's down in Washington, DC, shacked up with a guy twenty years younger, pretending he likes kale. He doesn't want to be forty-five? Okay. I don't want to babysit someone's inadequacies."

Evan nodded, flicked another fish. "I thought you both just worked too much," he admitted.

"We did. Because we didn't want to go home." Casper gestured to the office around them. "Crappy office, long hours, busywork, and bullshit policy? I would take it for hours and hours just so I didn't have to walk through that door and face another night of contemptuous stares."

Another fish disappeared into the little tray for Evan's phone messages.

"Or worse, disappointment."

Evan thought back to Sherri, to walking through the door at ten o'clock and feeling a twinge of irritation for a messy house or another plate of pasta in the microwave. How many times had he rushed out the door in the morning without thinking about Sherri handling four kids and the house without his help?

"I've fallen into the same crappy routine of my first... relationship," Evan said quietly. He didn't look up this time. "If I want to blame someone for this fight—for this pattern—it's all on me."

"Bullshit. It takes two people to fuck up a relationship."

A cold chill ran down Evan's spine. "I have to get home," he murmured, gathering his phone and keys. "I really have to get home."


HE SPENT the drive and the rush-hour traffic delays practicing what he might say. How to apologize for resetting their household in old, negative patterns. How to say, *I'm sorry I did this again and I swear it won't happen....*

Yeah, he'd made that promise before.

Despair filled his veins as he pulled up to the house. The lack of a car in the driveway surprised him as he parked there instead. The dash clock said six; they should all be home by now.

Lights were on. He could hear the television through the open front windows as he fumbled his keys in the lock.

Kent and Danny were sitting on the couch, Elizabeth in a side chair on her phone.

"Hi, Daddy!" she said, giving him a half smile and a little wave.

"Hey. Kent, how are you doing?"

Ever polite, Kent stood up and nodded. "Hi, Mr. Cerelli."

"I assume Miranda...."

"Yes, Miranda to the rescue."

His eldest daughter appeared, a soda in her hand. "Dinner's in, like, ten minutes. You want anything to drink?"

"No, thanks." Evan went through his routine—plug in his phone, take off his jacket. The living room occupants were pretending not to watch him, and Miranda went to sit on the couch's arm, next to Kent.

"Is, uh, is Matt home?" he asked, as casually as he could manage.

"Oh, sorry—that's the message I forgot to give you. He said he was staying up at Jim and Griffin's tonight," Miranda said blandly.

Evan's heart did a little jump. "Right. Did he mention how things were going?"

Miranda pulled her attention from the television. "No. Just said he'd be in touch."

DINNER WAS chatty, mostly due to Miranda taking control of the conversation. She kept the younger ones entertained and responsive while Evan ate his food mechanically.

Even this felt like a nasty rerun.

"So Daddy—since Matt has to be away tonight, do you need me to stay over and watch the kids?"

Evan pulled away from his little black rain cloud and looked over at her. For a second Sherri was sitting in that chair, half frowning at his distance.

"We can handle it," Danny said before he could speak. "Jeez, we're not babies."

"You can't drive yourself anywhere," Evan finally said. "I don't want you to miss work, Miranda."

She shrugged. "I checked with them just in case. I can work from home—or here, as the case may be. Is it okay for you to take the train?"

"Sure. Thank you for offering."

Miranda looked pleased at that, sharing a look with Kent. "Like I told Matt, I'm used to this sort of thing."

The food got unappetizing after that.


HE PUT Miranda and Kent in Katie's room for the night, unable to muster any sort of sternness about sex in his house. He figured fear of Katie finding out would put a damper on amorous activities.

Unable to go to bed without talking to Matt, he grabbed his phone and locked himself in Matt's office at the back of the house.

This was the center of his business—the neat files and stacks of blueprints, cameras in boxes, and endless pictures of locations they'd worked on. Evan knew a similar setup lived in Jim's office.

He knew they billed more and more each month. He knew Matt worked so hard on this business, put so much energy into having a career that mattered, that he felt pride in.

A career Evan had dismissed this morning before he walked out the door.

Evan dialed Matt's number, still not sure what he was going to say when Matt picked up. Fortunately—unfortunately—he never needed to come up with anything. Matt never answered.

# Chapter 14

"WELL, THIS is some bullshit," Jim said, pouring Matt another cup of coffee. It was four in the morning and no one had had any actual sleep for a full two days—except Sadie, of course, who didn't understand why no one had the energy to play with her.

They split shifts with Sadie, leaving Griffin as much time as possible to deal with the heartbroken Daisy.

No one looked good and no one had any idea how to fix this giant pile of shit.

"You should get some sleep." Matt poured an ungodly amount of sugar into the lead he was currently serving. "That baby's going to be up in about two hours."

Jim settled into the other kitchen chair, shaking his head. "I can't sleep. Between this drama and the rest of it, I close my eyes and everything starts playing like a Technicolor musical."

"You need to call the cops in Ashland."

"I will."

Matt sighed as he leaned his elbows on the table. He wanted a hot shower and ten hours of sleep, and he wanted to talk to Evan without needing to yell. He wasn't at that point yet.

He didn't know how to get to that point.

"If you're not going to sleep, then go to the office, package everything up, and send it off. Because we have other things to worry about right now."

Jim rolled his eyes. "While I am sorry for what Daisy is going through, it doesn't compare to a fucking murder investigation."

"Agreed, but you are retired, and even if you weren't, that shit is out of your jurisdiction," Matt snapped back. "We had a deal."

"And I will follow that deal, as soon as I get a moment to think." Jim got up, grabbing his coffee cup as he went. "You need to fight with someone, call your goddamn boyfriend."

He left out the back door, stalking toward the garage office. Matt watched him go with tired eyes.

Four missed calls from Evan. No messages. No texts. Matt didn't have a clue what that meant, and it certainly didn't help him figure out how not to be so pissed off.


HE GOT a few hours of sleep on the couch before noise in the kitchen woke him. Griffin had Sadie on one hip and a phone tucked against his ear as he attempted to navigate pouring milk into a cup.

"Yeah, no, I don't know." Griffin looked up and saw Matt in the doorway, a desperate expression coming across his face.

Matt went for the milk, since the little girl was just giving him a suspicious glare.

*Thank you,* Griffin mouthed before continuing the phone conversation. "Have you talked to the a-s-s-h-o-l-e today?"

After screwing the lid on the sippy cup, Matt offered it to Sadie, who looked at it like she was sure it was full of evil. Griffin took it, then handed it to the toddler.

Who started sucking away.

Matt tried not to take it personally.

"Well, if you do, tell him I quit."

Busying himself with a fresh cup of coffee, Matt heard shuffling and looked up to find Daisy entering the kitchen, her grief apparent in every line of her face.

"Hey, boss lady, you want some sugar with your coffee?" he asked gently, putting his arm around her shoulders.

She leaned against him, a light weight against his side. "Yes, please," she whispered.

They didn't move for a few minutes, just comforting each other next to the stove, in no hurry to break apart.

"Right, right. Let me know." Griffin's conversation was winding up. The refrigerator door opened and closed. "Call me later."

Daisy pulled away from Matt's side, peeking out from behind him.

"Momma!"

They ate breakfast at the table, Sadie in Daisy's lap, Matt and Griffin on each side. Griffin kept casting glances out the back window toward the office until Daisy patted him on the shoulder.

"Go bring him coffee or something," she said softly.

Griffin opened his mouth to put up a fight, but a few minutes later, he was gone, travel mug in hand.

"Jim's acting weird," Daisy murmured, a hitch in her voice. She absently stroked Sadie's hair as the little girl sucked on a piece of toast.

Matt couldn't shake his head fast enough. He knew what she was thinking. "It's not like that."

Daisy looked at him over Sadie's head with the saddest eyes he'd ever seen. "Are you sure?"

"Positive. It's a work thing." Matt swallowed back the full truth; that was as close as he could get without breaking a friend's confidence. "That's all."

Daisy nodded, twisting her daughter's hair around her fingers as the little girl made a giant mess of her toast.

They sat quietly, listening to Sadie babble, each locked in their own little world.

GRIFFIN FOUND Jim asleep in the easy chair, tucked under a heavy throw. The knocking, the door opening—Jim had slept through both, and Griffin was grateful. Grateful that Jim didn't hear his gasp or his string of curse words as he looked at what was spread across the desk.

The case against Tripp Ingersoll in all its god-awful glory.

He drank Jim's coffee as he rearranged the files and photos. It was clear what Jim's organization plan was—you lived with a man this long, you got his systems into your head, and it no longer looked slightly insane once you understood it.

The story laid out was sad and disgusting. Five girls, all away from home for the first time, all unaware that some asshole with no soul and no respect was going to end their young lives.

Griffin hated Tripp Ingersoll with an unholy passion.

And in the middle of this horrible story, he remembered how upset he was with Jim and how ugly this was going to be when he finally woke up. Because a secret like this.... Suddenly so much made sense.

Suddenly so much made him sick to his stomach.

He heard Jim stirring behind him, but he didn't turn. Griffin focused on the task at hand, didn't acknowledge the soft cursing, or his name, or Jim's presence in the chair by his side.

"It's chronological," he said finally. "Then each file is organized by evidence. I put Tracey's statement on top." Griffin patted the top of the stack. "What happens now?"

Jim cleared his throat. "I send it to the Homicide Department of the Ashland Police Department."

"Where the first girl died?"

"Yes. That's where Tracey went to school."

"Right, I read that." Griffin turned in his chair, trying to harden his heart before he looked at Jim.

The shame was not a surprise, nor was the embarrassment. The tears battered his heart, because Jim didn't cry. That was Griffin's role. "I'm sorry."

Griffin shook his head. "No, you're not. I mean, you're sorry I found this, but you're not sorry you did it. Please be honest." He rested his hands in his lap, refusing to touch Jim just yet. He needed time.

"You're right," Jim said softly.

"Does Matt know?"

"Yes. He told me to get rid of this—send if off and let it go."

Tilting his head to one side, Griffin smiled faintly. "That's not going to happen, is it?"

"I'm sending it off." Jim reached for him, but Griffin didn't move.

"What's it going to take? I mean—100 percent honesty here, Jim. What's going to put this case to rest for you?"

Jim rubbed his hand over his face. He looked… older, suddenly, and Griffin's heart broke a little. He played in the world of justice and cops and victims. He read the files and saw the pictures, but he'd never understand the pieces of Jim's soul that rested in all those cases over all those years.

"He has to go to jail," Jim murmured finally.

Griffin nodded. This time he reached for Jim's hand, twining their fingers together. He clasped his other hand over Jim's until he felt like he'd anchored his fiancé to the moment. "Do what you have to do, then," Griffin said. "Just finish it."

"Thank you." Jim closed the space between them and kissed Griffin's forehead. "Thank you. I'm sorry I didn't…."

"We can't get married until you're done, though. We can't—move ahead on other things," he broke in, voice wavering as his heart crumbled into little pieces. "I need all of you, not the parts that say yes because you feel guilty."

This was why Jim proposed. This was why he'd acquiesced to the baby talk.

Guilt.

"No, no—that's not why I...."

Griffin shook his head. He couldn't look at Jim anymore, not right now. "I love you, okay? And we're fine. We're just—paused."

Jim dropped his forehead to their clasped hands, saving Griffin the trouble of closing his eyes. They both cried a little while the faces of those dead girls stared up at Griffin from the desk.


MATT WAS still at the table when Griffin came back a few hours later. He looked like shit, a fact Matt did not comment on. They shared a glance as Griffin moved to put the empty cup in the sink, and then Matt realized just what happened.

"Griffin, Jim is just...."

Griffin shook his head. "I'm not taking it personally, don't worry about it," he said flatly before leaving the room.

Matt drank another cup of disgusting coffee, then watched his phone light up again without picking it up.

# Chapter 15

EVAN LEFT Miranda in charge once again, and took the train to the city with Kent. They didn't speak, didn't bother with small talk as the N rocked and rattled into Manhattan. Evan felt uncomfortable with all his family's dirty laundry laid out for this young man to see.

They parted at Forty-Second Street, walking their separate ways.

Evan added his daughter and her boyfriend to the list of people to apologize to.

Matt wasn't answering the phone, a fact that fueled Evan's strides to his precinct, jittering his blood more than all the caffeine in the world. He got the hint. It needed to be more than just a phone call. Evan figured he could get into his office, shut the door, and leave the most apologetic message in the world—hopefully prompting Matt to call him back.

Of course his best-laid plans fell to shit when he walked through the door.

The precinct with the lowest crime rate in the city was suddenly buzzing with a mugging and a break-in at a high-end dress shop. His phone started ringing as soon as he sat down and kept going until nearly five. Every time he picked up the cell to leave a message for Matt, someone else showed up wanting "five minutes of his time."

He gave them all ten minutes, a quiet despair at the back of his mind. *I have to fix this.*

At a loss, he took his cell into the men's room and tapped out a text.

*I love you. I'm sorry. Calling at six. Please pick up.*

He waited an hour, but his phone finally buzzed back.

*OK.*

AT SIX, Evan locked his door, shut off the light, and drew the blinds. Only his desk lamp stayed lit as he pressed the line for Matt's cell.

It rang and he waited.

On the third ring, Matt picked up.

"Hey," he said coolly.

Evan tapped his fingers against the desk. "Hey. How's everything at Jim and Griffin's? Is Daisy all right?"

"Fine—well, not fine. Everyone's kind of shitty right now," Matt said finally. He sounded exhausted.

"Do you need anything? I can, uh—I can drive up if you need clothes or whatever."

"I packed a bag."

Evan felt the world tilt a little. "Oh. Well—I wanted to apologize for what happened yesterday morning. That was really unfair of me to just dump that into your lap."

Matt didn't respond. Evan took a deep breath.

"Miranda handled everything, but uh—she shouldn't have to. Your career is important—"

"But not as important as yours."

"Matt, I never said—"

"No, you don't have to say the words when the actions speak for themselves."

"You're right—my actions said, 'You handle it, it's not my problem.' And I am ashamed of how I behaved."

He could hear Matt breathing—he could feel his anger through the line—and for a moment, Evan contemplated hanging up.

"Fine, you're sorry. What happens the next time? Because we both know there will be."

Evan felt frustration welling up. "Do you want me to quit? Because that's the only way I can guarantee this won't happen again."

Nothing.

"You pushed me to do this. You were in favor of me taking this promotion."

"Wait, so this is my fault?" Matt's tone was utterly incredulous. "I tell you to take advantage of a great opportunity, you decide that's permission to be a dick?"

"That's not what I'm saying!" Evan knew this was going badly. His irritation flared even as he told himself to shut up. "But we both knew what it meant before I said yes."

"So I should have been prepared for you to fuck me over like you did your wife."

Something painful and mean exploded behind Evan's eyes. "You don't get to talk like you knew her."

Matt laughed, cold and bitter. "I didn't know her, but I'm starting to understand her life."

The line went dead.

The urge to rip something in half with his bare hands overwhelmed Evan. After all their years together, some things were still off-limits. The children, Sherri—they were never weapons or pawns. Whatever flared and snapped between them, they kept it between them.

This was different. Ugly.

Because the worst part was Matt was right.


EVAN WENT home to Miranda folding laundry at the dining room table. She didn't say anything when he refused dinner in favor of collapsing on the couch. She brought him a beer and sat in the recliner, silent and yet so loudly judgmental, he couldn't even look at her.


HE DREAMED of Sherri and Matt, cold and fierce, refusing to speak to him as he pleaded and begged for a second chance.


AT BREAKFAST, Elizabeth kept staring at Matt's empty chair, refusing to engage in Miranda's attempt to make pleasant conversation. When Danny left without saying good-bye, Evan knew full well whose side his children were on.

"He's coming back, right?" Miranda asked as they stood at the front door.

Evan tucked his keys in his pocket, eyes averted. "Yeah. We just— we need a few days to sort something out."

Miranda crossed her arms over her chest. When Evan looked at her, he saw confusion and sadness playing across her features. It felt like Sherri judging him. It felt like a terrible warning.

"Okay," she said finally, scuffing her slippers against the entryway rug. "It would suck for the family to get all broken again. I mean—the kids don't need that, you know."

Evan swallowed a lump in his throat and drew Miranda into his arms. "Thanks, honey. I don't want it to be broken either."

EVAN SENT two texts on the subway, holding tight to a pole as he typed one-handed.

*I'm sorry.*

*Please come home so we can talk.*

He didn't get an answer.

# Chapter 16

JIM AND Matt sat in the office, each on their own side of the desk, not looking up.

They were in full work mode, the murder cases divided in half, with Jim taking the odd case out. Calls were made, information triple-checked, more evidence tucked into the files.

In an hour, the phone was scheduled to ring and a Detective Owens from the police department in Ashland, Oregon, would then be presented their case against Tripp Ingersoll. Off the record, of course.

Jim sent another document to the printer, then brought up the UPS website to schedule a pickup.

"Not that I don't love your company, but how long are you planning to stay?" Jim asked, typing in the address of Ashland's PD.

"I can leave if it's a problem," Matt said stiffly.

"I didn't say that. I'm just trying to figure out if you left your boyfriend or this is just a selfless act."

Matt let out a strangled laugh. "No such thing as a selfless act."

"Fine." Jim sighed as he turned to face Matt. "You left Evan."

"No. I just came up here to help you and it was perfectly timed with my boyfriend being a dick." Matt slapped a folder closed. "I needed a break, okay?"

Jim shrugged, the grit of overuse and a lack of sleep taking a toll on his entire body. "Fine."

They fell back into a tense silence, every movement a bit harder than necessary. A folder hitting the desk, a drawer yanked out, then slammed back in. A headache began to pulse behind Jim's eyes, each throb with its own name.

Lack of sleep.

Shame.

Anger.

Even the ticks of the clock seemed to mock the pain.

A sigh from the other side of the room stilled Jim's hands as he reached for a box to pack the files.

"Sorry. This is bullshit—I don't need to be fighting with you too," Matt murmured.

Jim turned the chair around, then slid across the floor closer to Matt. "Agreed."

"He keeps calling."

"That's a good sign."

Watching his friend carefully, Jim couldn't miss the depth of his sadness. It reminded him all too well of a night a few years back when two stupidly lonely and heartsore people sat next to each other on some barstools and wound up becoming best friends.

The tightness around his eyes, the downward pull of his mouth. The way his hands trembled as he pushed a pencil around the blotter.

"He doesn't leave a message," Matt said. "Just calls and hangs up."

"Maybe he doesn't know what to say."

"Well, that saves me from having an answer." Matt swiveled the chair to face Jim. "This keeps coming up. Not every day, not every month. But it's always fucking there."

The stack of files sat on the desk between them like punctuation to a ridiculous joke. Jim couldn't miss the metaphor.

"You told me to finish it—then pack it up and let it go." Jim kicked at the wheels of Matt's chair. "Maybe you should take your own advice."

Matt's head lolled to one side as he shot Jim a look of derision. "So lobotomies for both of us? Erase our memories?"

"No, but talk it out. Tell him how it makes you feel—"

"Your dead wife gets in the way of our relationship?"

"Don't start with that." Jim sighed as he stood up, stretching tired and aching limbs. "Maybe… maybe couples' therapy?"

Matt glanced up at him, his lower jaw actually dropped.

Jim heard the words come out of his mouth, then winced at Matt's expression. "Yeah, I heard it."

"Are you all right? Are you fucking delirious?"

A smile tickled Jim's mouth—exhaustion high, shields low. He started to laugh. "A yoga retreat?"

Matt glared until he started to laugh too. "Shut up."

"Kama Sutra Weekend for Couples. Phallic Pottery for Partners."

Tears started to leak out of Jim's eyes. He snorted, then fell back in the chair as he covered his face with both hands. "Poetry for Lovers," he got out before he dissolved into laughter again.

Nothing but the sound of choking and snickering filled the room for four or five minutes straight. Jim would look up, his gaze would meet Matt's, and they would fall into it again. Jim shook with the release. A near-hysterical edge buzzed to the sound, but it didn't matter. Maybe these were tears bursting out in a different form. If he couldn't cry or throw a chair through the window, he could let it out like this.


MATT WIPED his face with the sleeve of his sweatshirt. The thing needed to be set on fire at this point, as he'd been wearing it for over twenty hours. Sweat, tears, and the slick of emotional exhaustion permeated his skin and clothing.

Hot shower—he needed one of those. A full meal.

His kids.

Because fuck. *Fuck.*

The laughter trickled to a chuckle until he was sitting in the chair with his face in his hands. This wasn't just about a stupid fight with Evan. This wasn't even about Sherri's ghost—or the slot in the household that Matt so eagerly slipped into.

This was about going almost two days without talking to the kids, and the guilt started to choke him. Their kids—*their* kids. That was what Evan said. That was what those papers in the safety deposit box meant. But more than that, in Matt's heart, they were his.

Matt cleared his throat, choked on the tears still hovering. "I'm gonna go call my kids, okay?"


HE STARTED with Katie, because she was his girl. She picked up right away, a frantic swirl of words before he could say her name.

"What's wrong? Why aren't you home? What happened?" she asked. "Matt, you didn't leave Daddy, did you?"

"Calm down, please," Matt said gently. "There's a lot going on, but it'll be fine."

"Don't lie to me," Katie snapped. "Don't. I'm not a child."

Matt leaned against the garage, feet in the mud and his back soaking up the morning dew off the wooden shingles. Everything around him presented a sense of serenity, a quiet haven in the middle of trees and flowering bushes, the pool water lapping quietly. "We had a fight, but that's not why I left. My friends needed me, okay? That's all." The truth—with a lie woven through so quietly he hoped she wouldn't notice.

"You didn't call the kids," Katie said accusingly. "Your friends can't be more important than that."

He winced. "You're right. And I'm going to speak to them as soon as they're out of school."

"What about Dad?"

She wasn't letting him off the hook easily—which, if he was honest, was why he had called her first. "I'll talk to him too."

"Just promise, please?"

"I promise you, sweetheart. I'll make everything all right."

When Katie started crying through the line, Matt's heart broke.


EVAN WAS on the phone when his cell rang. He scratched out notes on a legal pad as the community board president complained about the recent mugging. The papers were running stories about how crime was on the rise in Midtown, something not borne out by statistics, and *this is how property values take a hit. Did Evan understand that?*

His cell vibrated wildly, and Evan almost ignored it, but it might be....

It was.

"Mr. Killian? I think I should come down and speak to you in person," Evan said quickly, sliding his finger across the strip and connecting the call.

"One second, please," he whispered to Matt before going back to his angry citizen. "Can we meet first thing in the morning?"

The real estate broker sighed dramatically but agreed. Eight at his office, first thing in the morning. Evan knew he'd have some serious public relations work to do and plenty of glad-handing, but anything to finish this call. He'd take Casper. It would be fine.

He hung up and immediately pressed the cell to his ear. "Matt... sorry about that."

"It's fine, I know you're busy."

Evan opened his mouth, then closed it. Coward that he was, he dodged around the words—and the sound in Matt's voice. "How's everyone doing up there?"

"Lots of coffee, very little sleep. Being cheerful for Sadie's sake is fucking exhausting."

And Evan knew that sound in his voice—way beyond tired, resigned. "I'm...."

"How are Danny and Elizabeth?" Matt cut him off. "I haven't called them, and I feel terrible about that." Matt's voice cracked.

"They understand you have to help your friends," Evan said carefully. He picked up the pencil and started to nervously doodle Matt's name under the notes from Killian's rant.

"I'll call them after school."

His heart sank. "So you're staying up there?" he asked. "For a few more days?"

*Please say no. Please come home.*

"Maybe. I don't know." Each word got scratchier and heavier until Evan felt the despair in his chest. "We need to talk."

The pencil dug into the paper until the tip broke on the curve between the *a* and *t* in Matt's name. "Then come home. Just—we can't do this over the phone. You'll feel better, the kids will feel better. Please," Evan said in a rush. "We can do this."

Silence stretched out between them, Evan's plea sitting out there in the middle, offering Matt a choice.

"Please," Evan repeated. "We can do this."

And that was it—that was what Evan hung on to. They wanted to do this, fought for it even when they were fighting each other.

"Okay. I'll be home by five."

Gratitude and relief rushed through Evan's chest. He covered his eyes with his hand, breathed.

Deeply.

"Thank you."

"We need—"

"I love you," Evan said firmly. "I love you."

"I love you too."

Then the call was disconnected.


AT FOUR Evan started clearing his desk. He'd talk to his sergeant about leaving early again, something that pained him—Evan didn't leave early; Evan didn't come in late. He fought against his natural instinct to stay.

Fifteen minutes later, a knock sounded on his door.

"Evan, sorry." Casper was already inside before Evan could call out. "Can we talk?"

Evan checked his watch, biting the inside of his cheek as he gestured Casper in. "Something wrong?"

"The mugging victim is holding a press conference with her lawyer," he said, waving his phone around like Evan could see what it said. "In about an hour."

Swallowing a curse, Evan stood up, momentarily at a loss for what to do. "Where?"

"Where she got attacked."

Now Evan swore. "Fuck. That's gonna look...."

"I know someone in her lawyer's office—he's a PR whore, and if I tell him I can get the captain down there to support her call for action, I think he'll say yes." Casper crossed his arms over his chest. "Better press than her standing there alone."

Evan grabbed his phone, clutching it in desperately clenching hands. A decision had to be made—a decision he didn't want to make.

"Call him. I'll do it," Evan snapped. "And if you can excuse me, I need to make a call."

Casper's expression was telling. Maybe sympathetic, but mostly knowing.


MATT WAS already on the road when the text came through. He'd showered, packed up his few belongings, and after hugging the entire population of the house, headed for Brooklyn.

The call with the Ashland Police Department had gone well enough. Jim looked slightly less troubled. Matt felt ready to leave. He needed to be home. Before the urge to find a bar and drown his sorrows became more than a reappearing bad habit.

As he pulled into the driveway, the very first thing Matt noticed was the lack of Evan's SUV.

When he grabbed the phone from the console, the message was not a surprise. But it was a disappointment.

# Chapter 17

ONCE UPON a time, the sight of Jim on the living room floor with Sadie—giving purple monkey a checkup with a giant stethoscope—would have destroyed Griffin's sense of propriety and left him a puddle of joy on the floor.

Now he just felt sick to his stomach.

Daisy, in a pair of his sweats that threatened to swallow her entirely, sat at his side on the couch, struggling not to cry. "I thought he was different," she said for the thousandth time.

Griffin squeezed her hand gently. "I know, sweetheart."

"I signed a prenup thinking this time—this time I wouldn't need it. I was so safe I signed the thing laughing." She bit her lip, a tear slipping out of the corner of her eye. "I'm safe, but I don't wanna be."

"F-u-c-k him," Griffin muttered, sliding Daisy into his arms.

He tried not to panic for himself, pushing down thoughts of his movie. Maybe it was the lack of sleep, but he was beginning to feel like the Carmen Kelly case—and everything surrounding it—was cursed. You think things are fine, you think you've figured out how to make everyone happy, and it falls apart.

Again.

Jim chasing Tripp Ingersoll. Daisy, first with Claus and now with Bennett. Griffin putting his eggs in other people's baskets.

The Kelly family movie.

His new play.

The two things meant to realign his career were in the hands of the douche bag who had broken Daisy's heart.

Déjà fucking vu.

"Potty!" Sadie announced, though from Jim's expression, it was a delayed call.

"Oh crap," Griffin said, but Jim shook his head.

"Nope, not that."

When Daisy started to move, Jim was already up, stain on his pants and Sadie in his arms. "I got it, it's okay. Cleaning I am totally comfortable with."

Griffin watched Jim go, then went back to snuggling Daisy—to find that she was staring at him.

"What?"

"I can't wait to see you guys get married," Daisy said, and then she burst into tears.

Griffin pulled her against his chest and decided to wait to tell her they were on hold for that happy occasion.

MAYBE IT was overkill, but Sadie Ames got a bath after her peeing mishap in the living room. She smacked her hands together in the bubbles, popping them and giggling at each sound. Jim dutifully brushed the purple monkey as was their ritual now—and he tried to ignore the fact that his pants had a giant stain on one leg.

He wanted a bath too.

"Dim?"

Jim stopped attending to the stuffed animal and looked down at Sadie. "Uh, yeah." Surprised at the attempt at his name, he dropped down next to the tub. "What's up, Sadie?"

"Dim." She smiled brightly, pointing one little hand in his direction.

"Yeah, I guess that's me. Dim."

He was glad Griffin had stayed downstairs.

Finished with the conversation, Sadie went back to her bubble popping. Jim just watched her, letting the quiet feeling of caring for her wash over him.

CLEANED UP and redressed, Sadie and the monkey decided to jump on Uncle Dim's bed for a while, while he ducked into the closet to change his pants.

And shirt.

And underwear.

He'd washed his hands three times, but he still felt like he was wet in a very undesirable way.

"Freeze!" he yelled the second before he disappeared. Sadie began giggling hysterically as she lay flat on the bed. "Keep freezing!" Jim yelled again, changing quickly.

He'd burn his clothes later.

In jeans and a sweater, Jim went back into the bedroom. He and Sadie had a moment of a staring contest, with Sadie hiccupping with the giggles.

"Unfreeze!" Jim said. Sadie didn't wait a second, jumping up to resume her bouncing.

"Uncle Griffin is a damn... darn... genius for inventing that game," he muttered, sitting on the end of the bed as Sadie used his beloved bed like her own personal trampoline.

GRIFFIN GOT Daisy to go upstairs and take a nap, maneuvering her away from the bar and the medicine cabinet. His shirt was wet, his heart hurt, and at some point he needed to call Bennett—that fucking lying asshole—and end their business relationship.

Even if they got back together, Griffin was done with trusting friends. And possibly all human beings.

Except, of course, for Jim.

He leaned against the doorjamb, watching Jim and Sadie on the bed. Sadie bounced and bounced as Jim made that purple monkey do the same. The pure delight on Sadie's face could cure cancer, Griffin imagined. She had no idea about the turmoil or the stress her mother was facing. All she knew was jumping up and down on a bed was the best thing ever.

Griffin walked into the room, smiling when Sadie saw him and squealed, "Miff!"

"I'm Dim, by the way," Jim said, extending his hand to Griffin.

"You're dumb, I'm annoyed. I'll remember that during our next fight," Griffin remarked lightly. He dropped onto the bed next to his fiancé.

"Can we schedule that for a long, long time from now?"

Sadie fell down to her knees, looking a little dizzy. Griffin opened his arms and she happily crawled to sit on his lap. They were a cozy little group, and Griffin's heart skipped a few beats.

"You're really good with her," Griffin murmured as he petted her damp, sweaty hair.

"I was thinking the same thing about you."

Griffin flushed with delight, leaning down to drop a kiss on Jim's forehead. Sadie sparkled at the sight, then mimicked Griffin's move. To Jim, to Griffin, and then to the monkey.

"Dim," she said dreamily, and Griffin started to laugh.

"You and me both, sweetheart."


SADIE, JIM, and the monkey fell asleep. Daisy didn't come out of the bedroom.

Griffin decided to act like an adult.

Downstairs in the kitchen, he found Georgia the housekeeper filling the fridge with food. Griffin caught her up with the new arrangements—temporary, he assumed. They needed toddler-type food and more milk and beer. Yeah. Probably more of that. Because it was hard to miss how they were down to nothing and Griffin hadn't had more than two in the past week.

Georgia made sympathetic noises and promised to come back tomorrow with what they needed. Did he want soup? Maybe a lasagna?

He made puppy-dog faces at her until she threw in homemade macaroni and cheese.

She left with a list and a very large check.

Soda in hand, Griffin headed for the back patio with his phone. He didn't want Daisy to hear this conversation, or Sadie. And if Jim was listening, he'd take over, driven by his alpha-maleitude. But Griffin was determined to do this himself.

Bennett's private number. Griffin pressed the little phone icon as he sat on the deck chair, the evening breeze ruffling the trees overhead. In a way, he hated to soil this beautiful spot with the about-to-occur harshly spoken conversation, but maybe it would anchor him.

"Griffin," Bennett said quietly as soon as the line picked up. "I'm so glad you…."

"This is a business call," Griffin answer briskly. "I need to sever our relationship going forward, but we still have postproduction on the Kelly project. I expect that contract to be fulfilled."

"If you could just listen to me." Bennett's broken voice didn't sway Griffin at all. He'd felt too many of Daisy's tears to give a shit.

"Business call—this is about the Kelly project getting its proper release. And you won't do anything punitive because of my relationship with Daisy."

Bennett made a wet sound. "I would never—"

"I'm going to take your word?" Griffin snapped. "After what you did? Everything you said to me was a fucking lie."

Then there was just the sound of crying.

"We're going to release this movie and then it's done."

"The play," Bennett muttered. "You still have that. I want you and Shane to have that."

"I'm not making money for you, asshole. No, wait—maybe I will. Then Daisy can take it in the divorce."

"Divorce?"

The surprise in Bennett's voice lit a fire in Griffin that singed everything in the general vicinity. "You don't think she's going to divorce you? You don't think that every one of *her* friends isn't pushing her to find a lawyer? She told me that you agreed—a lie is a deal breaker. A lie about fucking someone else makes the deal explode like a damn bomb. Stop acting so fucking surprised."

Bennett pulled himself together after that. Griffin could hear him breathing heavily and then clearing his throat. "I need to speak to her."

Griffin laughed at him. "No."

"That's her choice, not yours."

"Good point! Has she called you? Answered her phone? No? That's her choice."

"Then I'm coming up there—"

Griffin actually hit his palm against his thigh at that. Hilarious—this guy was fucking hilarious. "Please do. I'll watch from the picture window while my fiancé beats the living shit out of you, then throws you in the back of a police car. Hey, give me an ETA so I can call the press to make sure they don't miss a frame."

Griffin disconnected the call after that, then deleted Bennett from all his contacts. They were done, and when Daisy asked his opinion? Griffin was going to hand her a list of divorce lawyers.

# Chapter 18

MATT WATCHED Evan on the news, bookended by the twins, Elizabeth curled up against him. She hadn't left his side since he'd walked through the door, and was clutching at his hand so desperately he hugged her for a very long time.

For both their sakes.

"Is everything okay?" she whispered under the curtain of her hair and Matt's warm embrace.

"Everything's fine. Uncle Jim and Uncle Griffin needed my help with some important stuff. That's why I had to go up there."

The explanation seemed to surprise Elizabeth; she pulled back, her eyes wide. "But Miranda said—"

"Miranda made a very easy mistake," Matt said smoothly, catching her eye as she regarded him from the dining room. "But it's fine—I understand how that could happen."

Miranda rolled her eyes, but she didn't say anything.


"YOU NEED a ride?" Matt asked after dinner was finished and the twins' homework supervised.

"Nah. I'm meeting Kent two stops from here. We're checking out a beer garden!"

"Mmm, hipsters drinking imported brews and eating tofu sausages— please send me the address," Matt said, handing over her bag.

Miranda regarded him critically, hands on her hips. "Everything's okay here? I can leave?"

"You can leave."

"You're not going to move out again?"

Matt matched her stance and tone. "Once upon a time you'd have been cheerleading me out the door."

She tossed her hair, grown-up and still that willful teenager at the same time. "Well, that was before I realized you're the only person who makes decent tacos around here."

He smirked. "You like me."

"Ew, no." When she smiled and threw her arms around his neck, Matt kissed her noisily on the cheek.

After Miranda left, Matt picked up around the house. He felt like he'd been gone a month and not two days; everything felt slightly unfamiliar, like back when they lived in Evan and Sherri's house and not Matt and Evan's house.

The twins reappeared after homework, content to flop down on the couch with Matt again to watch television. No one mentioned Evan or when he was coming home. Elizabeth held his hand, head against his shoulder. Even Danny—stoic, quiet Danny—sat closer to Matt than normal.

*This is why I came back*, Matt thought. This was why, whatever he needed to fix with Evan, he would do it—because beyond loving Evan with all his heart, these kids were his life.

The door rattled a little after nine. Matt felt Elizabeth tense up and Danny shut down; he patted them both before slowly standing.

Evan walked through the front door. In one hand, his bag. In the other, a bouquet of red roses.


DANNY DIDN'T stick around. He mumbled good nights, then gave Matt a half hug bro thing that Evan took to heart. His only son wasn't affectionate like that, particularly without provocation. Elizabeth lingered, clearly afraid to go to bed.

"Everything's fine. I told you. Go to bed," Matt murmured to her. "I'll see you in the morning."

"Pancakes sound good, right?" Evan said, fake cheerful. Elizabeth hugged them both again, then headed upstairs.

That was when Evan realized he was standing in the middle of the foyer with a bouquet of flowers, alone with Matt. "Hi," he started.

Matt looked at the flowers, then at Evan, and shook his head slowly. "We really need to talk, don't we?"

THE ROSES sat between them on the kitchen table. Evan had a plate of food to ignore. Matt had his hands wrapped around a beer.

"I know I already apologized, but I want to say again—I was an asshole and I'm sorry," Evan said evenly, more to the pork chops and less to Matt, whom he still couldn't look in the eye, apparently.

"Right, you said."

"And I wish I could have left earlier today, but—"

"We saw the press conference," Matt said shortly. "And I got your text."

"It just—popped up. Casper asked me to...."

Matt got up and stalked to the fridge.

"I don't know what you want me to say."

*I need to go shopping*, Matt thought, ignoring Evan for the moment. *We need orange juice and mustard.* Matt took out another beer despite the fact that he hadn't finished the one at the table.

"I'm not here to guide you through this, Evan." Matt opened the beer, leaned against the fridge because distance was still something he needed. "I thought we moved past this shit."

"Matt."

"We settled this. You and me, together. Our relationship, our rules. Then I find myself yet again having a flashback to your old life."

Evan's hands clenched. His gaze was pleading, but Matt drew the line between them. He had to.

"I said I was sorry."

"You think the flowers work like that?"

"I just thought—"

Matt kicked the bottom of the cabinets, spinning around to block Evan's face from his view. "You thought 'I'm sorry' and some flowers and what? A nice fuck and everything goes back to normal?" Matt slammed the beer down on the counter. "Your old bullshit patterns are not my problem."

"What about yours?" Evan asked, low and dark.

Matt turned slowly. "Excuse me?"

"Running to—"

Matt put up both hands. "Say it and I pack my bags."

Evan shut down like a robot with a switch flipped to Off. He sagged in the chair and dropped his head into his hands. "Oh fuck." He was shaking his head when he sat back up; he got out of the chair slowly. "I'm sorry. This isn't going the way I wanted it to."

Matt didn't say anything. He held his ground, hands flat against the countertop.

"This isn't about Sherri or you being her replacement. This is my shit that I dragged you into," Evan said, hands up like he was approaching a skittish perp.

"I shouldn't have left," Matt muttered. "That's on me."

Evan relaxed. He stopped a few feet from where Matt stood.

"Because it hurt the kids, and that's never my intent," he finished. "I'm realizing that I can't punish you without doing the same to them, and that is bullshit. It's what my parents did, and I won't do it with ours."

The words slipped into his speech so naturally that he felt each one in his chest.

*Ours.*

Evan's face crumpled. "I'm—"

"Don't say you're sorry, and throw the flowers away," Matt sighed. "I'm going to bed."


MATT SHOWERED for an inordinate amount of time, standing under the blistering-hot water until it ran cold. And then he stood there for a little bit more.

The bathroom smelled like them, the bed just beyond the wall calling him to sleep but not promising him any rest. A hundred years ago, Matt Haight would have packed his shit up and been gone. No—no, he'd never have been here in the first place, putting down roots so deep he didn't know how to be away and angry or even protect himself. "Not here" felt like a punishment, even if being back in the house was a punch in the gut.

He toweled off, rubbing his face over and over until his eyes stopped leaking.

When Matt opened the bathroom door, he found the bedroom dark, the air-conditioning whirring. Normal, like any other night, Evan a lump on his side of the bed.

Matt had half a mind to storm downstairs, but he couldn't do it. He imagined the kids waking up to him on the couch, and somehow that hurt ten times as much as getting into bed with Evan.

And when had that ever been an issue?

Matt threw the towel into the hamper, then made the short trek to the bed. Evan didn't move as Matt slid under the covers. Didn't speak while Matt thumped his pillows until he found a comfortable groove.

"I'm turning in my resignation tomorrow," Evan said suddenly.

Matt shut his eyes. "No, you're not."

"Not compromising my family for this job—not you, not the kids."

"Evan."

"I ruined Sherri's life and there's nothing I can do about it," he murmured. "Not doing it to you."

Matt willed himself not to move, willed his muscles to stay locked and unyielding, but he had no willpower, no way to stop his hand from sliding across the bed to touch Evan's hip. "Taking away our careers isn't going to solve the problem," Matt said sadly. "We'll find other ways to hurt each other. That's what happens."

Evan sighed; Matt heard him hit the mattress with his fist.

"Whatever I have to do, I will," Evan said finally, and Matt squeezed his hip in response.

*You can't change who you are*, Matt thought. *And neither can I.*

# Chapter 19

THE NEXT morning Matt made pancakes. The children looked lighter, happier, with him there. Evan drank his coffee quietly, soaking up the conversation. He didn't participate, but he kept his eyes on Matt's every movement.

Matt insisted he not resign, but every passing second pushed Evan to do something. If he looked at his career right now, what was he doing? Was he making a difference? Was he a public relations device with no future except to have his picture taken and his name brought up when someone accused the NYPD of a lack of diversity?

He hadn't wanted to be a poster child when they first came to him, and yet what was he if not that?

There were three texts on his phone, all from Casper. News outlets wanted to speak to Evan today to discuss his appearance on the news last night. His initiatives and plans for the Midtown Precinct. Evan knew the question they'd all ask, and it had nothing to do with a mugging.

*What's it like being the NYPD's first out gay captain?*

*Like being a straight one, except I come home to someone of the same gender* was not the answer they wanted.

Faintly sick, Evan finished his coffee. "I'll take them to school," he told Matt at the stove. The kids were in the living room gathering their backpacks, so they had a second of privacy. "It's going to be a busy day, but I'll try to call."

Matt nodded.

Evan didn't want to leave like this. He touched Matt's face, stroked two fingers against his jaw before leaning into his personal space.

Everything was slow—the lean, the tilt of his head, the wait for Matt to stop him—but their lips touched and Evan felt grounded to the earth again.

Matt slid his arms around Evan's waist; he kept him close but not tightly held, trailing his palms down Evan's back.

The kiss felt like a homecoming—a slow flick of Evan's tongue, the scrape of teeth against the bottom of Matt's lip. Evan pulled away, searching Matt's face for something—anything—that told him he could walk out the door right now and still come home to this. Them.

"Come have lunch with me. After one," Evan said suddenly. The fear poked at him, provoked a breathless request.

Matt closed his eyes, ducked his head to rest their foreheads together. "Yeah."

*SO WHAT'S it like to be the NYPD's first out gay captain?*

Three interviews, three questions, the exact same wording. Evan gave a politely terse "I'm honored to serve the public," and Casper pushed for the next question. Evan managed not to quit on the spot.

All morning and afternoon, he thought about Matt. Everything from their first meeting until this morning, every little stupid thing from the bad and terrifying to the beautiful and perfect. The thought that he might lose that like he had once before filled him with a fear he had not experienced for a long time.

And he was a man who had existed in a place of fear most of his life.

*I love you.*

He texted it once an hour until they were scheduled to meet for lunch.

"GOOD DAY," Casper said as they made it back to Evan's office. He slid off his jacket, making himself at home in Evan's visitor chair. "Some of those interviews weren't entirely hideous."

"I hate it. I don't understand how you work with these people all the time," Evan muttered, going through the stack of messages on his desk. His phone sat front and center, though, capturing a glance from him at least once a minute.

"They're just doing their job, Evan. Some of them are even convinced their words make a difference."

"They should write about how people in this neighborhood have it easy."

"God, please don't ever give quotes that I don't preapprove." Casper looked at his watch. "You want to get lunch?"

"No—thank you, but Matt's coming and we're going out." Evan sorted the stack of papers into two piles: Later and Much Later.

"Oh."

Evan heard the flat tone and looked up. "What?"

"Nothing. I just thought you two...." Casper looked uncomfortable. "Never mind."

"You thought what?"

Casper shrugged. The easygoing mood broken, he got up and reached for his jacket. "I should get back to my office. I'll send you copies of the interviews once they're up."

Evan didn't have time for Casper's moodiness or his bitterness about his breakup with Tony. He was more interested in saving his relationship than going over the postmortem of someone else's.

The nasty thought made him flinch a second later. He grimaced. "Casper—thank you for today. I'll talk to you tomorrow."

Casper paused in the open doorway, seemingly interested in saying something else, but nothing came out. "See you tomorrow," he said eventually, then turned—directly into Matt's path.

The two exchanged muttered greetings Evan couldn't hear from his desk. He watched Casper hurry away and then Matt walking into his office with a frown.

"Is he always here?" Matt asked.

"He works here." Evan kept his voice even as he got up. "But he's gone now. Where do you want to go?"

Matt lifted a bag from Evan's favorite deli back in Brooklyn. "Let's eat in."

They set up their food on Evan's desk. It was a touching gesture, one that gave Evan hope even as he felt like even more of an asshole because of the flowers.

No thought, automatic.

"Extra pickles," Matt said, unwrapping Evan's sandwich.

"Thank you. For this and for coming down to have lunch."

Matt didn't look at him, just fussed with the salads and forks, tiny plastic containers of mayo. "Napkin?"

"Matt."

Their gazes met over the desk, and Evan poured every ounce of sincerity into his smile. "Thank you."

"Gotta eat," Matt answered, but Evan felt like maybe they were making progress.

Eventually they settled into the rhythm of them—talking about the kids, Matt updating Evan on everything regarding Bennett and Daisy. Evan shook his head through the entire story, dropping the rest of his uneaten sandwich onto the paper.

"I would never imagine he could do that," Evan said softly. "He seemed so focused on her, so happy when we were together last summer."

Matt shifted uncomfortably in his chair. "The fact that it was a guy—I don't know. It just pissed me off more. Like, everyone shoves that stereotype in your face if you've been with women and men. What if you change your mind? And you tell people that's bullshit, but...."

Evan heard the note of concern. He felt it himself.

"What Bennett did wasn't about his sexuality, though. It was a choice to cheat and break his vows."

"So the hottest woman in the world gives you a lap dance, all you feel is...."

"Embarrassed, because at my last job, I would have had to arrest her."

Matt laughed. "What about the hottest man in the world?"

"Same answer. I'd hate to have to arrest you," he said lightly, holding a breath to see how Matt would react to the flirting.

He got an eyebrow raise. "You're just trying to butter me up so I'll give you my brownie."

Evan shrugged, eyeing the small white bag on the edge of their lunch mess. "Brownie for a lap dance?"

"Now you're just yanking my chain, Cerelli."

They shared a smile—a secret one. Evan knew what it meant when Matt's smile curled a certain way, when his eyes took on a mischievous shine. The best part for Evan, though, was that they were in a public place. They were definitely flirting. Playing for a moment's respite.

Nothing was solved, but God, Evan needed that smile right now.

"Brownie for a lap dance—and then you'll have to cuff me." The words didn't flow in any sort of sexy way. Evan sputtered a little on the word *cuff* and he could feel his cheeks getting warm. He had to look away when Matt hooted quietly.

"You are just the literal worst at sex talk."

Evan frowned. "I was good at phone... thing."

"See, when you have to call it a thing...."

They laughed again and Evan felt something settle in his bones.


"SEE YOU at home," Evan said when the ringing phone became a constant interruption. It wasn't a question.

Matt nodded as he gathered up their lunch remains—and stole Evan's brownie in the process. "I have calls to make when I get back, so I hope you have strong positive feelings about Greek food."

"That's fine." Evan took a breath as he delivered the next bit of news. "It might be late. Eight, eight thirty."

The bag of garbage dropped into the can next to his desk. Matt's expression stayed neutral. "Like I said, I have calls. Things to catch up on. I'll be in my office."

Evan walked him to the door. The squad room seemed to turn and look in unison before going back to their work. In his head, Evan balanced on a line between public Evan and private Evan—all while trying to make sure his boyfriend was at their home later tonight.

"If I can get out earlier, I will," he murmured, but Matt smiled.

"Come get me when you're home," Matt said. He made no attempt to kiss Evan, who experienced a sense of sad gratitude when Matt walked away.


MATT CHECKED in with Jim after a few hours of calls to clients. Jim hadn't heard back from the Ashland PD, but according to the UPS website, they signed for the evidence two hours ago. Before Matt called, Jim had basically paced the entire property when he wasn't getting a crash course in parenting thanks to Sadie.

Griffin and Daisy were outside by the pool, apparently arguing about her getting a divorce lawyer, as Jim reported to Matt from his perch in the kitchen—mostly to make sure no one got shoved underwater.

"You gonna end up on my couch again?" Jim asked sternly.

Matt leaned back in his chair until he found the comforting creak. "No. Because I hate the way the kids felt when I did," he sighed. "I don't want to fight in front of them, but—they lost their mom so violently and so suddenly.

There's this whole abandonment thing, I think...," Matt started, then stopped when he realized Jim was laughing through the phone. "What?"

"You're such a good dad."

Matt bounced in his chair, squeaking it until Jim was concerned it would break. "Why is that funny?" he asked, a twist in his chest at how pleased that made him feel.

"Because you're Matt, and when we met, I'd have been concerned about your ability to keep a fern alive. Hell, mine too. Which is why we're friends. And now you're all Dr. Whoever on TV, being a mature... dad. It's weird."

"You're weird."

"Hey, you're my role model. For, uh, when I'm in your shoes." Jim coughed dramatically.

"Seriously?"

"What are your feelings regarding Uncle Matt?"

Matt sniffed. "There's a branch in my eye."

"Such an incredible asshole."

"Can I call godfather now?"

AFTER THE chat with Jim, Matt cleared up his desk, then headed upstairs. It was almost ten, the kids were in bed, and Evan was still not home.

Matt pretended this was a test from the universe.

Shower, bed. Tomorrow was another day to hoe the row of being a responsible adult.

# Chapter 20

EVAN MANAGED not to slam the front door as he got home two hours later than he intended to. Casper had forgotten to mention the meetings after hours, the ones Evan needed to attend to keep the major real estate players in Midtown happy. Evan had tried to keep his temper, because they were friends and he knew Casper was still struggling, but Jesus Christ.

Why today.

He blew through the first floor as fast as he could, dropping his things in their proper places before heading upstairs.

Matt's car in the driveway was reassuring. The touches around the first floor—dinner in the microwave, the back door locked, the lights out—told him Matt had gone through the nightly routine already.

Half the ride home, Evan had been freaking out that he'd come up to an empty driveway. Or Matt and his bags sitting in the living room, waiting to end things once and for all.

He wouldn't do that to the kids, Evan knew, but he really wanted Matt to be waiting—and staying—for him as well.

In the bedroom, he heard the shower going and relaxed another tick. He followed the sound, debating his next move.

Should it even be a move?

When he reached the bathroom door, he made his decision. Through the thickening film of steam on the shower door, Evan saw the water trickling over his lover's soft skin and strong muscles, and he acted without conscious thought. Evan stripped out of his pants and T-shirt, then slid back the shower door.

Matt didn't turn around when Evan climbed into the shower. He kept his head tilted out of the stream of water, his arms against the tile, open and inviting. Evan said nothing, just ran a hand down Matt's back. It made him shiver with anticipation, even in the middle of all the steam.

Evan stepped in behind him and stood still, listening to the thundering patter of the water as the spray bounced off Matt's chest, splattering back to hit his own skin.

Then he slid his splayed fingers slowly around Matt's waist and down over his thighs. He ran the tips of his thumbs down the length of Matt's dick and leaned in against his back, breathing in the steam as Evan's lips teased behind his ear.

Goosebumps rolled over Matt's skin. He melted against Evan, breath catching as they connected. Evan rubbed his dick up against Matt's beautiful round ass. He pulled Matt suddenly back at the hips so they were pressed tight against each other. He moved his lips lazily along the back of Matt's neck.

This wasn't their normal routine, but Evan felt challenged to do something. If he couldn't show up on time, he was going to let Matt know how he felt with more than words.

Murmuring Evan's name, Matt reached behind him with both hands, finding Evan's hips and pulling him closer. He tilted his head to give Evan access, pushing back with intent that Evan responded to with a snap of his hips. Water splattered over them as Evan mouthed the warm expanse of Matt's shoulders.

He trailed his fingers up over Matt's stomach while cupping and gently squeezing his cock with his other hand. The familiarity of Matt's body soothed Evan, sparked his nerve endings. His anticipation built; he ground his hips, tugging and stroking Matt, their movements getting rougher, sloppier.

He wanted more.

Evan slid his hands onto Matt's shoulders, then down along his arms, ending with his hands resting on top of Matt's, holding them against his hips. They rocked against each other, Evan angling his dick between the globes of Matt's ass. When Matt bent forward and pushed back, Evan groaned.

He knew what Matt wanted, and suddenly it connected in some sort of wild and ridiculous meaningful act in his mind.

The rub of flesh against flesh nearly shorted out Evan's brain—he knew what he wanted to do to Matt, for Matt—but God. He bent his knees slightly, then stroked up, and they almost went down in a pile under the rush of water. The sensation became a need as he slowly pulled away.

Matt reached back for him, but Evan was already on his knees.

"Mmm, what you do to me," Evan whispered as he turned Matt toward him, guiding hands on his hips. He looked up, the water hitting Matt's shoulders and raining down on Evan.

Whatever dizzying hunger was running through Evan's mind and body, Matt's expression captured it perfectly. Evan didn't wait—not when they were both starving for it. He swirled his tongue against the head of Matt's cock, brazenly maintaining eye contact.

Evan ran his lips along the length of Matt's dick. Matt's dick. *His* dick. The thought came into Evan's head unbidden and fierce.

With that in mind, Evan curled his tongue around the head and let the hard wet rod slide deep into his mouth, then drew back, flicking his tongue against the underside, licking him slowly. He repeated the pattern over and over, his gaze fixed on Matt's face, watching his every gasp and moan.

Evan knew Matt was holding back—he could feel the strain of his body, the rigid way he held his breath—but Evan knew all the secrets. He knew how to suck the smooth head in just enough and hold until Matt trembled. Evan wrapped his fingers around Matt's dick as he lavished attention on the head, rolling his hand up and down the length. Then he hungrily sank back down, sliding his other hand behind Matt's ass, working a finger inside to tease his hole.

Evan tightened his lips against Matt's cock as a grin filled his face. Matt's immediate physical reaction was too obvious to ignore. Evan pulled back again and pressed a kiss to the base of Matt's dick, wriggling his finger farther inside.

And then Matt took over. Evan opened his mouth wider, teasing with his finger, letting Matt have his way.

Matt dropped his hands to either side of Evan's face, shivering. The water had started to go cold, but Evan didn't blink or complain—he just relaxed his jaw, his throat, and stared up at Matt with absolute adoration.

He didn't have to wait long. Matt was long past being patient or gentle. He gave over to Evan's acquiescence and pumped his hips with abandon.

IN BED, Evan didn't want anything. Matt kept sliding his hand between Evan's legs, but Evan pushed him away gently, distracting him with kisses.

"Why don't you want me?" Matt whispered, biting at his jaw and neck. "I want you."

"You had me," Evan croaked in return. He took Matt's hand and wrapped it around his throat.

Matt laughed and moaned, pressing Evan into the mattress. "Is this so I'll forgive you for being late?" he teased, tightening his grip just enough to make Evan raise his hips off the bed.

Evan shook his head, lost for a second in the combination of Matt's blanketing heat and the dizzying relief of Matt's hands on him. "No." He coughed a little, the burn of his throat worth it. "Maybe."

"Jerk." Matt moved his hands then, surging up over Evan and pinning him to the bed. "Maybe I don't forgive you yet."

Evan struggled just enough for Matt to know he was game. "You trying to fuck another apology out of me, Haight?" he whispered.

Matt's smile turned wicked.

# Chapter 21

THE BAR crawl wasn't anywhere Matt wanted to be. Another GOAL activity for the young single and those reentering the dating scene. Two new recruits to the organization were supposed to be chaperoning the thing, but one broken leg (skiing) and a concussion (jerk who didn't want to stop punching another jerk) had left GOAL in need of responsible adults.

Apparently Evan owed Jesse a favor.

So Matt, in jeans and a tight black sweater, hustled a group of twenty-two singles, as they grew more and more inebriated, through the streets of the Village.

"Where now?" he asked Evan, who was soberly manning the map, checking locations on his phone.

"Around the block—we'll be sampling tequila."

A "woo-hoo, yeah" chant started up behind them. Matt wished he had a nightstick. "How is this an intelligent exercise in meeting people? There's going to be a bunch of hookups; then everything is awkward at the barbecue next month," Matt whispered. "Not to mention the NYPD's finest lurching down the street, publicly intoxicated."

"Well if you hate it, show up at the events committee and make suggestions," Evan said, giving him the cross father look.

"Oh, you did not just tell me to put up or shut up."

"No," Evan said slowly. "I told you to come to the meetings and make a suggestion."

"Here's my suggestion—herding drunks around is a shitty way to spend a Saturday night."

At the next bar, Matt found a corner table while their group bellied up the bar—literally—for a tequila sampling.

"I know how this ends," Matt muttered to himself as he flipped through his phone. He and Jim had exchanged e-mails earlier in the day; Jim would be flying out to Oregon to meet with the Ashland PD himself, in hopes of pushing the department to reopen the case of the murdered coed, with Tripp as their prime suspect. Griffin was staying at the house with Daisy and Sadie, and Matt had promised to check on them while pretending he wasn't checking on them at Jim's behest.

He got it—he totally did.

On to sports scores, he missed the arrival of Casper Vaughn. One second Evan was chatting with the bar owner. The next Evan was crowded into the corner with Casper.

Overdressed douche bag.

Matt stuck his phone in his pocket, then sauntered over to where the two men were talking. "Oh hey, Casper, great to see you," he said, wrapping one arm around Evan's waist. "Getting back on the horse— that's fantastic."

Evan elbowed him in the stomach, but Matt didn't let go.

Casper looked at him like Matt had just crawled up from the sewer. *Yeah, son, the feeling is entirely mutual.*

"Actually I came to see Evan—didn't realize you'd be here," Casper said, faux pleasant. "Don't you usually babysit on Saturday nights?"

"Our kids are out with family. We have a free night to uh...." Matt smirked as he rocked his hips. "Have a good time."

"Glad you could join us," Evan cut in. "We need to move on."

Evan wrestled out of Matt's arms, then walked away, map and phone in hand. "Let's go, everyone," he called.

Casper and Matt shared a long, nasty glare, then followed Evan and the crowd out the door.


EVAN FINALLY cracked and had a drink at the final bar, a hole-in-the-wall with a band and the world's smallest dance floor. They shared a beer, Matt glued to Evan's side like a predatory bodyguard, his hands wandering as far as Evan would let them.

Evan... let him.

Everything felt like a test: how long Evan talked to Casper, how affectionate he was with Matt in public, what they discussed about work. Rather than feeling pressured or uncomfortable, Evan leaned against Matt with absolute abandon.

If this was a test, Evan was acing it.

"How drunk do you have to be before you'll let me kiss you in public?" Matt whispered in his ear. Evan was leaning on a cocktail table, Matt behind him, their bodies lined up perfectly. "And how much have you had so far?"

"Half a beer," Evan whispered back.

"Is that the answer to both?"

Evan pushed back with his hips just slightly.

Matt bit the back of his neck. "How many drinks will it take for you to dance with me?" Matt asked as he pulled Evan onto the dance floor.

"Half a beer," Evan said, clumsy in Matt's arms until he stopped trying to lead.

They slow danced on the floor, ignoring the alcohol-fueled hookups happening around them, some of which might indeed lead to awkwardness at the barbecue.

Evan didn't care. His body buzzed with desire, his brain shorted in and out; he kept trying to find a memory to match this moment from before, and nothing came to mind.

Nothing.

This was theirs.

"How much... how drunk do you have to be," he asked Matt breathlessly, "for me to fuck you?"

Matt pulled back, his face a picture of utter surprise as he blinked at Evan. "What?"

"We tried that time and it didn't work." *Because I was too afraid and too stupid*, he thought. "But it's different now."

He didn't answer—no, Matt gave him the most perfect answer in the world. He kissed Evan on the dance floor, tender and romantic.

MATT DIDN'T want to say good-bye to Casper—he grabbed Evan's hand, threw a hundred at the bartender, then headed for the door. The car was parked at Port Authority, which meant a cab ride to Midtown. Evan let himself be pulled along, pliant and smiling like he had a secret in the backseat of the taxi.

"What's gotten into you?" Matt said, twitching with how much he wanted to be home, now.

Evan shrugged, rolling closer to him as they sped along Tenth Avenue. "You, repeatedly," he deadpanned. "Now it's my turn."

MIDNIGHT. THE kids were in bed, Miranda asleep in Katie's room. Evan in the lead, they tiptoed through the house, stopping periodically to kiss, sloppy and frantic, on the stairs.

"Hurry up," Evan laughed, pulling away. "It's sure as hell not happening here."

He pushed Matt through the bedroom door, then shut it behind them. Turned the lock and leaned back against it, reaching for the top button of his shirt.

"Take off your damn clothes, Haight," he said, already pulling his shirt out of his pants.

Matt didn't go for finesse or a sexy striptease. He pulled the sweater over his head, wrestled out of his jeans without looking away from Evan's face. Evan let everything fall away—clothes, inhibitions.

When he was naked—but more importantly, when *Matt* was naked—Evan pushed off the door.

"Bed?" Matt asked, grinning with anticipation.

Evan shook his head. "Up against the wall."

He arranged Matt the way he wanted: facing the wall, braced against his arms. He dropped to his knees and pushed Matt's legs apart just enough to reach his goal. Evan pressed his lips to the base of Matt's spine, then traveled down between his asscheeks and wetly kissed his hole.

This wasn't new. Evan listened to Matt curse, then buried his tongue inside his lover. In, pull back, in again. He tightened his fingers against Matt's hips, holding him in place.

Matt's entire body was moving, pushing back greedily to get more and more of Evan's mouth.

Evan dropped one hand to his lap to take his dick in hand. He stroked in time with the plunge of his tongue until he was moaning into Matt's skin through the spit-slick kisses.

When they were both moaning and moving with abandon, Evan found his moment to pull back. "Here or on the bed?" he asked, moving his hands over Matt's back and hips and thighs.

"Bed," Matt moaned out, still rocking back against Evan.

MATT LAY facedown on the bed, shaking and rubbing against the bedspread in his frantic need to come. Evan straddled his thighs, aggressively sliding two fingers and too much lube inside him. Matt loved this, needed it, but the next step kept his body tense.

"Calm, calm, easy," Evan murmured, increasing the thrust of his fingers. "Just let me in."

Matt couldn't stop moving.

"Up now, like that." Matt knew how to rise on his knees, slope his back and open his hips. He saw Evan in that position, knew the gorgeous sound Evan made when Matt pushed inside him.

He didn't make that sound—he jerked and flinched at the pain.

"Do you want me to—"

"Don't stop," Matt moaned as he pressed his face into the comforter. His voice shorted out with one last fevered gasp. After that it was just silence save their shared labored breathing as Evan breached Matt's body with his own. The pain was overwhelming, the burn seemed to rip him in half—but he didn't say no or stop or jerk away. He relaxed as much as he could, breathing in a slow rasp against the mattress.

Evan was as gentle as he could be, pushing his dick inside slowly and carefully. He wrapped an arm around Matt's chest, anchoring them together, and whispered in Matt's ear. "God, I love you, you feel so good. Let me in, baby, let me in."

"Yeah," Matt breathed. "Oh...." Something caught in his psyche; the hot stab of pain turned into pressure, which turned to an anxious thrust backward. His breath stuttered, his entire focus on his growing sense of need.

Evan waited, his movements small and gentle until he seemed to sense Matt's readiness. "Now okay? I'm gonna...," Evan muttered, and then everything in Matt's world tilted sideways.

His arms slid until his chest hit the bed; Evan went with him, the angle and penetration taking Matt's breath away.

"Yeah, yeah, yeah." Every time Evan slammed forward, the word forced itself out of Matt's mouth. Matt heard the bed hitting the wall; he heard his own voice crying out in sheer surprise at how much he never wanted it to end.

Evan drew a sudden deep breath, eased back a little way, then pushed in with a shudder until Matt jerked like something lit up inside him.

"...ohgodohgod," Matt babbled, fingers scrabbling against the comforter as he fought to push back and pull away from Evan at the same time.

"Oh God," Evan gasped. "Oh fuck, Matt."

Yes, so good—Matt was in total agreement, but he couldn't speak beyond moans or register anything past the painful, beautiful ache from Evan's pounding movements. He crossed the place, that line in his head where he ceased to be anything but in this moment.

His whole body rocking, writhing, Evan grew louder, more vigorous, as Matt lost himself in the sensation, listening as Evan's words got more filthy, more brutal, until they dissolved into guttural sounds.

Matt was floating in bliss, even as his body was taken and lovingly bruised. He absorbed it all, greedy and passive at once. The urgency to come peaked as Evan jerked hard against him, the sensation of his orgasm shaking Matt loose.

Evan reached around to stroke his cock once, twice, and then Matt lost himself in coming.


HUMID, HOT, sticky—Evan would normally be up and out of the bed, eager to wipe off and be comfortable. But for now, the sprawl against Matt's back felt too perfect to disturb. He pulled out slowly, soothing the murmured hitch in Matt's breathing with a kiss against his shoulder.

But he still didn't get up.

"Too heavy?" he whispered, arms tight around Matt's chest.

"Yeah, but don't move," Matt answered, his voice hoarse and quiet.

Evan didn't move.

They lay there until the cooling of their bodies made them both twitch and Evan couldn't delay the inevitable. "Stay here," he said, sliding off Matt's muscular form with reluctance, and onto wobbly knees.

"No argument."

In the bathroom, Evan snapped on the light. As he removed the condom to tie it off, he caught sight of himself in the mirror.

He looked debauched and... smug.

Biting back a laugh, Evan threw the condom into the trash can, then washed his hands with the cloth next to the sink. He knew there would be a conversation when he got back into the bedroom. He knew they had issues to work through.

But right now, he felt so fucking buzzed and satisfied and—in love with Matt.

WHEN EVAN returned with a washcloth, Matt was far ahead of him. He had stripped and remade the bed and cleaned up and was putting a pile of sheets in the hamper.

"How long was I in there?" Evan asked, wrapping his arm around Matt's middle. "I thought you were down for the count."

"Second wind," Matt replied. Truth was, once the afterglow started to wear off, he'd felt a little uncomfortable. And not just because his ass hurt.

Did that just happen—as fucking amazing as it was—because Matt was jealous and Evan felt guilty?

Evan rocked his hips against his ass. "Again? I might need some sugar or something to boost my energy."

"That's okay, Casanova." Matt pulled away. Not angrily, not even because he was uncomfortable. More that he needed to talk (they needed to talk) and he didn't know where to start.

"Are you sorry we did that?" Evan asked suddenly, his voice taking on the sharp quality that had been plaguing them all too often lately.

"No." Matt turned around, now very aware they were naked with the lights on and about to slip into a tense conversation.

Matt sat down on the bed, wincing at the pull in his lower back.

Evan's face went tight.

"No, I'm not sorry. I'm just a little… I don't know. Too old not to notice that this came along at a really weird moment for us."

Evan dropped the damp washcloth in the hamper. He walked a few paces before settling down next to Matt. "Maybe it was that beer," he started, a little smile crossing his lips as he attempted to make a joke. "And maybe it was me just trying to concentrate on the good parts and not the bullshit."

Shaking his head, Matt ran both hands through the sweaty mess of his hair. "I don't like bullshit, Evan. I don't want it to be fights and fucking, because that's not who we are."

"No, we're not." Evan leaned into Matt's side so they were shoulder to shoulder, thigh to thigh. "We won't be."

The silence wove around them, not entirely uncomfortable. Matt blew out a sigh and Evan slid his hand into Matt's.

"Casper Vaughn is a dick and I don't like him," Matt said eventually.

"We work together," Evan said, tightening his grip on Matt's hand. "But we don't have to see him outside of that if you don't want to. He's going through a lot right now."

Matt's insides squeezed with tension even as he kept his hand relaxed. He looked at where their fingers were entwined and thought about how it felt perfectly natural. Grounding.

*I don't care*, Matt thought, but he nodded. "Sorry. He just rubs me the wrong way."

Evan sighed. "Yeah. He's been off lately. This breakup with Tony really messed him up."

"Maybe he hooked up with someone at the bar crawl," Matt said hopefully, and Evan laughed.

"Extra awkward at the GOAL barbeques."

*Don't care. Let him go sniff around someone else.*


THEY GOT under the covers eventually, and Evan clamped on to Matt's body like he was physically keeping him in bed lest he try to escape.

"We're okay, right?" Evan asked when the lights were out, his head on Matt's shoulder.

A beat too long and then Matt turned in his arms, landing a kiss gently on Evan's mouth. "We're gonna be okay," he murmured.

# Chapter 22

GRIFFIN OPENED the door to find Bennett on his doorstep, a spray of pink roses in one hand and a teddy bear in the other. Everything about Griffin's sharp-dressed former friend seemed subdued: black clothes, subtle expression. All the flash gone, or at least tucked away.

Griffin contemplated slamming the door in the man's face. "Can I help you?" he asked instead, cold as he could manage.

Bennett shifted nervously. "I'd like to speak to Daisy."

Griffin gave him the stink-eye. "She said I should let you in if you showed up," he spat. "If you upset her, I'm going to punch you in the fucking face."

"Understood," Bennett muttered.

Griffin stepped to the side and let Bennett in.

When he turned around, Griffin found Daisy standing at the bottom of the stairs, wringing her hands in front of her. "Let's go outside to talk. Sadie's sleeping," Daisy said primly. "Griffin, would you mind...."

"I'll take care of her."

SADIE WOKE up while Griffin was reading a book at her bedside.

"Miff," she said, rubbing her eyes.

"How about you, me, and the monkey take a walk?"

Walking with Sadie was slow going. She liked to pick up rocks and leaves and sticks, not to mention the occasional piece of garbage. It was similar to having a golden retriever. Griffin pulled a little red wagon behind them in case she got tired or found treasure under a pile of lawn clippings.

Right now, only the purple monkey enjoyed the ride.

They traveled up ten houses, then across the road to the opposite ten.

"Hey, nice flowers," Griffin said, directing her to a cluster of tiny purple blooms. They weren't on anyone's property as far as he could tell, which meant fair game.

"Ooooo, pwitty," Sadie cooed, getting down on her hands and knees to look a little closer.

Griffin took the moment to stretch, look up and down his street. Neighborly nosiness abounded: The Grennigers were trying a new lawn company. The Costas were repaving their driveway.

Did Mr. Blatt get a new car?

That's when the dark sedan caught his eye.

This wasn't a sedan type of neighborhood. Everyone drove an SUV or a minivan, with the occasional Volvo or MINI Cooper thrown in.

Black sedan, tinted windows.

Across the street and two houses down from his and Jim's place.

A little chill disrupted Griffin's thoughts.

Someone was sitting in a dark sedan across from his and Jim's house.

"Hey, Sadie, let's go back and have cookies, okay?" he said, reaching down to pick the little girl up.

"Kay." She had handfuls of purple flowers but clearly no objection to heading home for a snack.

Griffin held her close as he hurried across the road, pulling the wagon with his free hand.

At the mailbox, Griffin bounced the wagon onto the walkway. He stopped for a moment, looking over at the sedan one more time.

The motor gunned suddenly. Then it peeled out and sped off in a haze of exhaust.

Spooked, Griffin ran into the house, leaving the wagon behind. Sadie protested the bumpy trip inside, then started to yell for her monkey.

"One sec, Sadie. One sec."

Griffin slammed the door behind him and finally took a deep breath.


"YEAH, I didn't see who it was, but it spooked me," Griffin said, giving Jim every detail he could think of. He paced around the living room with the phone pressed to his ear as Daisy and Bennett sat on the couch, just far enough apart to avoid any contact. They looked as worried as Griffin felt. "It was clearly watching our house. And when I noticed it, it took off."

"You couldn't see who was driving?"

"No. I mean—windows tinted that dark. It freaked me out."

Jim didn't say anything for a long time. "I want you to arm the security system."

"Done."

"I'm calling Matt—"

"No, don't do that. We can handle it. Uh—Bennett's here."

Jim swore.

"So yeah, two big strong guys, and Daisy has Mace, and Sadie's pretty lethal when she whips Legos at your head," Griffin joked weakly. "You're gonna be back tomorrow, right?"

"Let me see if I can change my flight."

The adult in Griffin wanted to say *don't worry, it's fine*, but something in his soul reacted strongly to Jim being here sooner rather than later.

"Okay." Griffin stopped pacing. "Who do you think it could be? Like, I expected you to tell me I'm crazy, but instead you're totally feeding my hysteria. Which is very unlike you."

The sigh over the line didn't do anything to steady Griffin's nerves. "Maybe just press 'cause Daisy is staying there," he said, all neutral in a way that was not Jim-like at all. "I'll scare them away."

"I did that already. What do you really think it is?"

"We'll figure this out when I get home."


GRIFFIN AND Daisy stayed in the master bedroom with Sadie curled up between them. Bennett was on the couch with Mace and a baseball bat.

No one slept except the baby.

# Chapter 23

ASHLAND, OREGON, sat right over the California border, surrounded by some of the most beautiful mountains Jim had ever seen. The small town bustled around him thanks to the nearby college as Jim followed the GPS directions to the police station.

A detective named Howard Beech met him in the parking lot as Jim stretched in the warm sunlight.

"Detective Shea?" the man asked. He was a burly middle-aged guy in a gray sports jacket and Ray-Bans.

"Retired, but yeah," Jim said, extending his hand.

"Let's go talk," Detective Beech said, leading Jim into the brick building of the Ashland PD.

A small tan conference room housed a table, four chairs, and the box of evidence Jim had sent ahead, spread out and marked with tiny yellow sticky notes. A box of pens sat on a stack of legal pads.

"You need some coffee?" Beech asked as Jim sat down.

"No, thanks." Jim gestured to the painstakingly put together files. "So, what do you think?"

Detective Beech let out a snort of laughter as he settled across from Jim. "No small talk, eh?"

"Sorry." Jim put his hands up and tried to relax. It didn't work. "I'm just anxious."

"How long you been retired?"

"Three years." Jim settled back, resting his hands on the table.

"This guy won't let you sleep, huh?" Beech began pulling folders out of the pile, finally flipping one open in front of him with a *thwap* against the table.

"I can't get him for the Seattle murder, but maybe I can help you close some cases instead."

"I'm sure this is for my benefit." Detective Beech shot him a wink. "All right, Jim, let's break this down."


COFFEE BECAME necessary at about the forty-five-minute point. A uniformed cop brought them sandwiches and water two hours after that, but Jim couldn't sit down as he drew the time lines for Tracey's lacrosse team schedule and the murders. Every single one lined up. It was so clear, in clean strokes of black and red and blue, that Jim almost couldn't breathe.

How had no one seen this?

"No one saw it 'cause even if they did, he would have had an alibi," Detective Beech said. "You think the girlfriend wasn't covering for him?"

"We couldn't break her alibi for him," Jim said with a sigh. He turned to face Beech, who sat at the table. "She never even wavered."

"So his master plan is to only kill when Tracey can back him up. That's some kind of sick asshole right there, pardon my language."

Jim sank into a chair, weary to his bones. "Sick and organized. Thinking about his cover story before he does it."

They ate in silence, each man caught up in his thoughts. Jim's gaze kept darting to the pile of folders, as if he could see the pages and read each line all over again.

"How'd he get them to go with him?" Jim asked as he dropped his napkin into the waxed white paper.

"Good-looking kid, nice car. Manners." Detective Beech spat out each word. "None of these girls saw him as a threat."

Jim rocked in the chair, feet braced so he didn't roll away. "At night? In the parking lot of a store or a bar?"

"Hitchhiking maybe."

"I didn't see that in any of the interviews with friends and family."

More quiet, but Jim could feel them both processing the information.

"You remember that case up in Canada—the serial killer with the pretty wife," Detective Beech said suddenly.

Jim felt his jaw tense. "Good-looking guy, nice manners, nice car— his girlfriend in the passenger side," Jim murmured. "Holy shit."

IT WAS dark when Jim walked out to his car. Behind him, Detective Beech barked into the phone, talking to the detective from the town where victim number three went to school. The past hour had seen the office staff of Ashland Police Department copying and scanning all the materials, e-mailing them out, then packing everything up and labeling them for each of the departments that had an unsolved case with Tripp's fingerprints all over it.

If he had to skywrite the evidence to get their attention, he would.

Jim tried to put a label on what he was feeling: relieved, euphoric, satisfied. Mostly he felt exhausted.

Running low of energy.

He just wanted to go home.

Detective Beech hung up, and Jim stopped to turn around. They stood under the weak light overseeing the parking lot.

"You gonna stay at the hotel?"

Jim shook his head, putting one hand on the back of his neck to stop the spike of pain. "Jackson County Airport. I need to get home."

"All right, but you drive carefully. Those bags under your eyes are dangerously close to needing a building permit."

Extending his hand, Jim smiled. "Thank you for your help, Howard."

"We're gonna get this son of a bitch, don't you worry."

At the airport, Jim settled into a chair and waited for the boarding call for his flight to Salt Lake City. From there, he'd catch another plane to LaGuardia before the car service brought him home. Every cell of his body was struggling to stay functional; he wanted to shower and eat Georgia's food and make love to his fiancé and forget Tripp's existence.

Finally. He just wanted to be free of the weight of it.

His part was over. Detective Howard Beech, who smelled like peppermint and Old Spice, would take twenty years of experience and his easy-going manner and escalate the matter from Jim's brain to active law enforcement.

The other detectives would soon have everything they had found. The FBI would be contacted. Jim would sit back and let it go.

He closed his eyes and tried to concentrate on home, and not Tripp behind bars.

HIS PHONE rang as they sped away from the airport, Jim dozing in the backseat of the car service's black sedan. He didn't look at the caller ID, just answered as an automatic reaction.

"Mr. James Shea?" an unfamiliar woman's voice asked.

"Uh, yeah. Who is this?"

"My name is Lucy Fraser. I'm from the *Oregonian*."

Jim's brain tried to catch up. He sat straighter, pressing the heel of his hand into his eye. "Right—um, what can I do for you?"

"I've gotten some information about a murder investigation regarding the deaths of several Oregon college coeds about seven years ago...."

Jim was wide-awake. "Excuse me?"

"Are the police looking at Tripp Ingersoll for these murders?"

His throat closed as he took a gasp of air. "I'm retired," Jim said as calmly as possible. "I have nothing to do with active police investigations."

"You're the one who brought the information to the attention of the Ashland Police," the reporter said quickly, as if sensing Jim was about to end the call. "Is this because you couldn't secure a conviction in the Seattle case?"

Jim clenched his jaw tightly. "Lose this number or I'll report you for harassment."

"Or does this have to do with publicity for the upcoming movie—"

Jim disconnected before she finished her sentence.


TWENTY MINUTES later, he got three texts from Ben.
*Tripp's lawyers rescinded deal.*
*What's going on?*
*Jim, call me.*


FINALLY JIM arrived home, bleary-eyed from a trip with three separate legs and the weight of Tripp Ingersoll's case on his shoulders. He threw his bag on the bottom of the stairs and opened his arms for Griffin.

"Tell me what's going on," Griffin whispered.

Jim hugged him tight enough for his breath to catch, but nothing filled Griffin with fear like Jim's next words.

"Tripp knows I'm the person who gave the information to the police."

# Chapter 24

EVAN HUNG up with Matt, disturbed by the conversation they'd just had. Someone staking out Jim and Griffin's house? They'd talked to local police, but with so little to go on and few resources in the rural community, Matt and Jim had made the decision to send Daisy and Sadie back to the city. At least at the penthouse, they were sure of the security.

Evan sent a quick text to Griffin: *Here if you need anything.*

When his door opened, he looked up with some annoyance.

Casper.

"We're past the knocking thing, I see," Evan said, only half joking.

"I thought we were." Casper was always a smooth dresser, but today he'd outdone himself. He looked like he'd fallen out of a high-end men's magazine.

"You on camera today or something?"

*Got a tank?* Griffin texted back.

"No, but thanks for noticing." Casper shut the door behind him and Evan swallowed a sigh.

"Did we have a meeting?"

Casper came up short at that; Evan's tone clearly was not welcoming. "No, but I think we need to talk."

Evan texted Griffin again. *You and Jim are welcome at the bunker if you need a place to stay.*

Putting his phone to the side, Evan looked at Casper with his most patient expression. "I have a few minutes, sure."

Sitting down, Casper pulled a serious expression. "I'm worried about you, Evan."

His phone buzzed. Evan got distracted, then looked back at Casper. "What?"

"After Saturday night—I just can't keep quiet anymore. Matt's behavior was shocking and inappropriate. You were in front of fellow officers."

"Who were drunk and grinding and off duty." Evan tried to wrap his brain around Casper's train of thought. "Besides, what the hell did he do? We danced a little bit—neither of us were drunk or inappropriate."

*Oh, have times changed*, Evan thought. *How I've changed.*

Casper sat back in the chair. "You have to be aware of the gossip about him," he said, shifting and looking anywhere but at Evan. "He's a liability, Evan, as much as you don't want to hear that."

"Is this a joke?" Evan felt his hackles rise with each word out of Casper's mouth. "Are you kidding with this bullshit?"

"He reflects on you, Evan. You ever think he's why you're stuck in Midtown South?"

"No, I know exactly why I'm at Midtown South. Because I'm a token and you put the token in the safest, least problematic place so he doesn't fuck up and embarrass you."

"Or you put the guy with the boyfriend whose ass got booted out of the NYPD for misconduct somewhere no one will bring it up."

"You don't seem to have a problem." Evan stood slowly, splaying his hands on the desk. "I think you should leave."

Flustered, Casper stood as well. "He's bringing you down. You need a better person at your side, Evan. You need someone—"

It dawned on Evan then what this was about. He didn't even try to stifle the laugh, rude and loud, that escaped his mouth. "Someone like you? No—thank you, but no. I'm not in the market for a relationship designed to please other people."

Casper headed for the door, his face flushed and his mouth twitching with unspoken words.

"And Mr. Vaughn, just so you're aware, I'm going to call your superiors and inform them our collaboration isn't working."

A sneer came over Casper's face. "I'll be better off. Watching you dumb yourself down for the constituents makes me sick."

"Get out of my office," Evan snapped.


EVAN STEWED for the next few hours. He worked, had a meeting, called Matt, texted Griffin—all on the edge of throwing a filing cabinet through his fucking window.

It wasn't even ego. He would tell Matt tonight that he was absolutely right about Casper. He would even take the "I told you so." It was more that he had thought Casper was a friend, someone in a similar life situation to Evan, someone he could help move on after a breakup. The reality of their friendship being a lie, that Evan missed all the signs… his feelings were hurt.

And then there was the overwhelming anger, because fuck that jerk for speaking about Matt like that. How dare he? How dare anyone?

When the powers that be came to him before the test, before all of it—when they questioned his relationship with Matt—Evan had threatened to quit. His job meant the world to him, but he would quit for Matt. He would also punch Casper in the mouth if he ever heard Matt's name on his lips again.

"Asshole," he muttered, reaching for his phone.

A knock at his door: his sergeant, with a concerned look on his face.

"What's up?" Evan asked, putting the receiver down.

"Building by Bryant Park got vandalized. Lots of damage."

Evan cursed. He expected to hear from the community board president any second in that case. "Anyone hurt?"

"No, but uh—the person who called it in was a James Shea. He mentioned your name."

*Bryant Park? Jim?*

"Shit. I think I know whose office got hit." Evan got up and was around his desk in a flash, moving for his suit jacket. "I'm going to go over there. I have my phone if you need me."

# Chapter 25

EVAN MOVED through the chaos on the street. Three patrol cars, a fire truck, EMS. Gawkers and rubberneckers crowded the entrance of the building. Evan was already on the phone.

"Nora? Could you get me another car down to 1140 West Forty-Second Street? I need some crowd control and someone moving the traffic through so we don't wind up with a mess at rush hour. Thanks."

He flashed his badge and got waved through.

The elevator was locked to go only to the floor in question, the rest of the building already evacuated. When the doors opened, Evan caught a whiff of smoke and bleach.

Another flash of his badge, this time to the patrolman stationed at the entrance.

"What happened?" Evan asked, looking through the mess, trying to find Jim or Bennett.

The patrolman walked him over to the cordoned-off area. "Everyone came in late today. The upper floor was fine. But they smelled smoke, so they called 911. Fire department puts out a few waste can fires, then they realize the place had been wrecked before the fire."

Evan nodded through his explanation. "Arson squad?"

"Already here."

"Thanks." He started to walk toward the sound of voices but paused. "Hey, when the detectives get here, tell them there are security cameras all over the place. Make sure they get the feed."

Evan kept walking. He heard Matt's voice.

"WHAT THE fuck happened?" Matt asked, pacing around the farthest office, one of the only spots not destroyed by the fire or vandalism. Out there, accelerant over the rugs and desks, a sharp, heavy object taken to walls and windows, the fires—it was almost a total loss. "How did none of the alarms sound?"

Jim didn't say anything. His face was drawn and tight; he had his arms folded over his chest, not offering anything to Matt as he ranted.

"Matt?"

Hearing his name, Matt ducked out of the small office to find Evan walking carefully over the wreckage. "What are you doing here?"

"Got the call. It's my precinct." Evan gestured for Matt to head back to the office.

"Jim, thanks for letting me know."

Jim nodded, then reached in his pocket for his phone. "I'm gonna call Griffin and go upstairs, see what I can figure out."

When they were alone, Matt couldn't help pacing.

"Did you pull the security feed yet?"

"No," Matt spat. "There isn't any. Someone shut off the cameras. The sprinklers didn't activate, the silent alarm—nothing."

In all his time doing this, he'd never had a break-in. Never vandalism or damage—nothing. This infuriated him—to see the destruction of property and peace of mind around him.

"Inside job?"

Matt had thought of that. But he trusted their crew. He and Jim had investigated them thoroughly before hiring them, and they were good judges of character. But history had taught him that for the right money, most people would give up their mothers. "We have to look at my people, and Bennett's," Matt said with a heavy sigh. He pulled at the collar of his shirt. "I have to see who worked on this gig specifically."

"You get me names, I'll run them," Evan offered, but Matt shook his head.

"I already did that."

"I have access—"

Matt put his hand up, regarding his boyfriend with a "really?" expression. "So do I."

Evan opened and closed his mouth. "Please tell me you didn't just admit to having access to police databases."

"I didn't admit to anything." Matt pulled out his phone. "Let me call Eddie."


EDDIE, WORKING on a job uptown, freaked out a little about the vandalism. He took a cab down and met them in the lobby. "Matt, I'm so sorry," he said, joining them in the corner for an impromptu meeting.

"Not your fault, at least I hope not," Matt said grimly. "You did the final walk-through."

"Right." Eddie stuck his hands in the pockets of his jeans, shifting from foot to foot. "With Alex."

"The temporary guy," Jim put in.

Eddie nodded. "We checked everything, did the list, signed off on it."

Matt narrowed his eyes as he watched Eddie. Something was up. He knew his employee, and he'd never seen this level of anxiety. "You personally checked everything," Matt said, without the question mark at the end. "With your own eyes."

Eddie dropped his gaze.

"Oh shit," Jim sighed.

"Alex came recommended," Matt said, looking over at Jim.

"By Eddie."

All eyes turned to the young man. Cracking him wasn't even going to require work.


"I'LL HAVE him picked up," Evan tried again, but Matt and Jim were already half a block away from the mess, trying to find a cab.

"Or I'll go talk to him and find out who he sold the codes to, which will take about a quarter of the time," Matt snapped.

Evan put up his hands, dodging pedestrians on the corner of Fifth and Forty-Second. "I'm asking you to let this be a legal interrogation."

"We get lawyers involved in this and we'll never figure out who did this."

"Matt, think about what you just said. Jim, help me out here."

Jim said nothing as he stepped into the traffic and hailed a cab.


ALEX DIDN'T put up much resistance in the end.

Matt and Jim were terrifying enough, but Evan felt confident that his badge loosened the young man's tongue. He sat on the floor of his Inwood apartment, hands over his face.

"I haven't worked in fourteen months," Alex muttered, sniffling between words. "I needed the money. Eddie didn't know what was going on—I swear to God. He thought he was just helping me out."

Jim shared a look with Matt.

"What happened?" Evan asked, sitting across from Alex. He tried to keep the young man's attention on him and not the glowering twins on either side of him.

"After I got the job, I was at the bar down the street with Eddie, and this girl started talking to me after he left. She said she had a friend and he, uh, needed some information."

Matt let out a heavy sigh and walked around the small living room. Jim—well, Evan looked up and saw Jim was frozen, intent on Alex's shaking form.

"Did she say why he wanted the information?"

Alex shook his head.

Biting his tongue, Evan exhaled. "So this woman tells you she'll pay for the information. How much?"

"Five thousand dollars for the security codes in the office, another grand for me to disconnect the sprinklers."

Matt made a disgusted sound from across the room.

"Just tell me his name, the guy who paid you," Jim said suddenly, set on full glower, imposing his sheer size over the kid's still form.

"He didn't give me his name. Just a bunch of cash. We met out at Newark Airport. He flew in from Canada and—"

Jim interrupted, a note of anger in his voice that made Alex cringe and Matt snap to attention. "Where in Canada?"

"Um, Toronto. We met in the United lounge."

"Matt" was all Jim had to say.

Matt was already doing a search on his phone. He turned it to Alex after he found what he wanted. "This the guy?"

Alex squinted at the picture, then nodded. "Yeah. His hair's different and he's gained some weight, but that's him."

Evan leaned over to see what Alex was looking at. His stomach dropped when he saw Tripp Ingersoll's face staring back at him.

# Chapter 26

EVAN RETURNED to a crime scene in chaos. The press had settled at the front of the building, already updated on the situation. Multimillionaire Bennett Ames was the victim of a break-in and possible arson.

"Erin, it's me again. I need crowd control at the entrance," Evan snapped into his phone as the press on the fringes recognized the police captain in their midst.

They turned around and focused their attention on him. Half the press corps wanted to know if crime was on the rise in the neighborhood and the other half wanted to know if this had to do with Bennett and Daisy's divorce.

Evan paused to take a deep breath before waving his hands to get their attention. "I have no comment at this time. We'll schedule a press conference at the precinct when we have more information."

Behind him, he heard the siren of a newly arrived car.

"Contact the press office for information," he said before turning and heading for the sidewalk.

A black-and-white had taken Alex in for booking while Jim and Matt met Evan back at his office. No one talked. It seemed like they were all stewing in their own concerns.

Evan slammed the door, shaking up the quiet.

"So you've been illegally investigating Trip Ingersoll," Evan said, trying to keep his anger in check. "That's something."

Jim didn't sit down. He stood with his legs apart and his arms crossed over his chest. "I was gathering information, which I then shared with the police who have jurisdiction over one of the murders. What they choose to do with it is not my concern."

"Right." Evan flopped in his chair. "How'd he find out what you were doing?"

"A reporter called me on my way back from Oregon." Jim slumped the tiniest bit. "There must be a leak in the Ashland Police Department," he said. "What concerns me the most is that if he was coming back from Toronto, that means he met with his wife, Tracey." His mouth slid into a tight line after that, and Evan flexed his hands into fists until the urge to punch something passed.

"We need to make sure she's all right," Matt offered, but Jim didn't say anything.

Evan pulled everything together, tucked it all neatly into his game face. "I'll call the Toronto PD. Jim, just write down everything—how you contacted her, where you met." Evan pushed a pad and pen in Jim's direction. "I'm going to call the FBI as well, just to give them a heads-up. Let's see if we can contain this."


THEY COULDN'T contain it. The damage done to Bennett's offices started a round of front-page news. A new resident—famous, rich, able to afford the best security—the victim of a deranged stalker or disgruntled ex-employee or maybe just another example of this neighborhood going to hell.

Most of the papers kept their histrionics in that direction, but the *Post* had a hatchet job on all of them so thorough that Matt knew it was personal. His own checkered past was the lead, with a bit on Jim being sued back in Seattle and Evan's personal relationship with "one of the suspects."

Matt was a suspect?

Fuck them.

Matt burned with the shame of having his past thrown up again, and watching Jim and Evan get thrown under the bus pissed him off to no end. He hid in his home office, brooding and alone, ignoring calls from Liz and Vic, even his old partner, Abe.

Not again. He didn't want any of this again.

Evan didn't even bother to promise to be home. With Casper gone from his PR liaison role, Evan was managing the press deluge with personnel loans from the main office. None of them seemed to be able to direct the masses toward something less tabloid. No one gave a shit about parking or congestion, but this was a story they could get extra mileage out of. Recognizable names, lurid details.

Jim was hidden at the penthouse with Griffin, Daisy, and little Sadie. Bennett stayed at a hotel down the street because Griffin refused to sleep in the same space as him. A few clients had put projects "on hold" for various reasons, but most of their base was still gung ho. Matt made calls for hours, remained charming even though he wanted to punch a wall.

Then there was the brass.

Evan didn't tell him, and that was the rub. He had to hear from Helena.


HELENA BREEZED into Evan's office with two humongous cups of coffee and Shane, who was carrying his computer. She had been classified "not on active duty" as the NYPD tried to woo her into picking something else instead of resigning.

So she decided, as announced to Evan, that she and Shane would assist him during this incredible clusterfuck.

"What do we need?" Helena asked breezily, setting Shane up on the sofa and giving herself a corner of Evan's desk.

"Statements clarifying that this isn't some incredible soap opera full of melodramatics. A cloning machine and one of those thingamajigs from *Men in Black*." Evan took the proffered coffee and fell on it like a starving man.

"I'm on the statements, but if you can find a *Men in Black* thingy, I'll buy two," Shane said, opening his laptop.

"How about me?"

Evan looked Helena up and down. She was wearing a mint green lightweight suit and white blouse with pearl earrings and a gold watch. Everything about her was polished and perfect—like Casper, but at least he knew he could trust her with his very life. He picked up the phone and asked the operator to connect him with the PR department. He had a good idea for Casper's replacement.

"I'm not saying yes on a permanent basis," Helena said primly, sitting across from Evan with her hands folded on her lap. "I'm going to need to see a salary and benefits package."

Two senior NYPD officials showed up unannounced at his door a few hours later. Helena and Shane disappeared quickly. Evan offered them chairs and coffee.

They didn't want anything.

"Evan, we're a little concerned about this… problem you seem to be having," said Mr. Higgins. "This precinct is a positive in the shitstorm of crime in this city. You were given it so you'd have every opportunity to prove yourself. And now? All my good press from this place is in the shitter." His thick round face turned red with anger. "I have stories pointing out your relationship to the man involved with the break-in—"

"No, excuse me. Two things, Mr. Higgins—you knew about Matt when you approached me. Period. That hasn't changed. And he wasn't involved, as evidenced by the arrest of the man on accessory charges. He admitted to selling the codes."

"Yes, I know. We can read." Mr. Alsta pulled out a cell phone. "But there isn't much to combat when the Ingersoll lawyers are screaming that Jim Shea has been stalking their client, trying to frame him for murder."

"That's ridiculous," Evan snapped. He itched to point out they suspected Tripp in the break-in, but at this moment, he knew any speculation relating to Ingersoll would set the two men off.

"No, that's page four of the *Post* and page eleven on the *Daily News*," Mr. Higgins responded in the exact same tone.

"I want it to die down, Evan. I don't want to see Mr. Shea or Mr. Haight in the papers, on the investigation, quoted or otherwise mentioned," Mr. Alsta added. "And tell your boyfriend," he said, his dislike clear, "to stay out of the investigation. This has to stop being such a mess—a mess attached to your name."

Evan tightened his mouth into a flat line. "Of course."

# Chapter 27

"I TALKED to Howard over in Ashland," Jim said, shutting the study door behind Matt.

"What do they have?"

"The DA agreed with him. They're issuing a warrant for Tripp in the next twenty-four hours."

"He's in Toronto." Matt sank down in a chair, a headache throbbing behind his eyes. "Extradition, then—that's going to be fucking ridiculous."

He realized Jim wasn't answering, and when he looked at his friend, he saw the expression on his face—and panicked. "What is going on?"

"We haven't had a chance to talk about everything, but when I was in Ashland, Howard and I developed a theory," Jim murmured. "About how Tripp got all these girls into his car, why Tracey could always alibi him."

Matt's stomach fell to his shoes. "You think she's involved. Against her will, maybe—she left him…," he tried.

"Or his parents have cut him off during their own split…"

Matt picked up the thread dangling. "And what? They divorce, she gets money."

"She gets half of everything."

A mirthless smile slid across Matt's face. "Half of the stuff his parents won't let him touch. Like trust funds."

"They can keep him away from whatever they want."

"But they can't keep Tracey from it legally." Jim kicked the nearest object, a sturdy leather sofa that trembled under the force.

"Jesus Christ."

Matt had no idea what their next step was.

GRIFFIN THREW his unread book onto the couch, rolling his head on his shoulders until his neck cracked.

Jim and Matt were holed up in the penthouse study, frantically discussing things Griffin was not privy to. Which, on a good day, was annoying as fuck. At the other end of the apartment, Daisy and Bennett were "having a serious talk" in the sunroom. Even the baby was asleep, leaving Griffin to his own devices.

He had no devices.

Work was paused; the wedding was paused—his life was fucking paused and nothing could be done about it. He almost called his father, but what could he say? "Screwed up again, considering applying for a job at Banana Republic"?

Bored and agitated, Griffin got off the couch and wandered around the penthouse.

He walked past the study twice, stepping on the creaky floorboard just because. On the third pass, when Jim opened the door and then stuck his head out, he pretended to be surprised.

"Come in here. We want to talk to you."

In Bennett's study—done in a serious man palette, missing only the animal skin rugs—Griffin settled on the couch. Matt sat in the desk chair and Jim took the chair closest to Griffin.

"What's going on?"

"Jim and I have been talking to the Ashland cops today. A warrant's been issued for Tripp in Oregon, but no one thinks he's anywhere near there. We think he's in Toronto."

"Tracey," Griffin said with a grimace.

Jim nodded.

Griffin put his hand over Jim's. "Is she okay? Do we even know?"

Jim looked sick suddenly, white-pale and green around the gills.

"They're traveling together," Matt said softly.

Griffin's jaw dropped. "She went back to him after everything?"

Matt and Jim exchanged a glance that Griffin couldn't read. "We don't know exactly what's going on here."

They all sat in silence for a moment. Griffin contemplated the girl who couldn't seem to divorce herself from a dangerous, toxic man.

"And on the subject of what we can handle, we're thinking of heading to the Hamptons house," Matt said. "It's the only location where we know the codes are completely safe. Only Bennett and I know them."

"Oh, okay." Griffin rubbed his hands on his pants. "Should I—should I go? Or go home?"

"Not home. Not yet. You should go with Daisy and Sadie." Jim slid into the space next to him. "I'll feel better if you're there."

Griffin put on a brave face as he reached for Jim's hand. "You too, right?"

"Yeah, of course."

"Jim, you need to start carrying," Matt said. "At least until Tripp's found. I'm going to head out tonight, double-check the house. Then you guys come out tomorrow morning."

Jim made a noise of agreement as Griffin twitched at the thought.

"So fucking cloak and dagger," Griffin sighed, laying his head on Jim's shoulder. "I just want it done."


JIM TOOK Griffin into one of the guest rooms as Matt took over speaking to Bennett and Daisy about their plan. All of them looked like exhausted wrung-out pieces of shit, and Griffin had a whole second of guilt over using his big eyes and pout to make Jim go, "I'll be back—Griffin's got a headache. Let me get him into bed."

It might have been patronizing, but frankly, Griffin didn't give a shit. He wanted some quiet time with his fiancé.

"Gonna be honest, not in the mood," Griffin joked tiredly as he flopped on the bed.

Jim didn't laugh. He avoided looking at Griffin, prowling the room like a cat in search of an exit.

"You didn't do anything wrong."

"Yes, I did. I brought him back into our lives," Jim muttered.

"You're trying to help people. I bet those families wish they knew what happened to their daughters." Griffin frowned. "Maybe now they will."

Jim's smile was tentative, but Griffin knew he'd gotten through. He opened his arms for Jim to join him.

"We're going to get married," Griffin said soothingly as Jim settled against him. "That douche bag is going to jail. And we're going to be okay."

THE HOUSEKEEPER let Evan into the penthouse.

"In the study," he was told when he showed up at the front door and asked where to find Matt—easier said than done in the sprawling space.

"Hey."

Evan stopped in yet another hallway, turning to find Matt standing a few feet away. "Hey, sorry. I didn't have any clue where the study was."

"It's fine."

The stilted tone worried Evan. He walked toward Matt, who began moving away. They eventually settled into the study, both on the sofa, neither looking the other in the eye.

"So," Matt began. "Helena said you had some visitors."

Oh.

Evan took a breath, then let it out. Helena was either being chatty or meddling—he would address that next time he saw her. Right now, though, his concentration was on Matt. And how there was no way to say these things and not set off Matt's anger. "They want the press to settle down. They want me to restore order. They, uh—they want you and Jim out of the papers. You're bad press for the precinct."

Evan watched Matt's anger bloom, from his posture to the flush of his skin to the line his mouth flattened into. He braced himself for the explosion.

But none came.

"That didn't take long, to drag me into it," Matt said quietly.

"No, it didn't." Evan touched his arm. "We need to make a decision."

"Not right now."

Evan took Matt's hand in his. "When this is done," he murmured.

# Chapter 28

EVAN DRAGGED himself home at eleven. He'd sat next to Matt earlier as they called the kids—even Katie in Boston, where she was all but hopping on a bus to get home. They reassured them and kept a positive attitude, both of them faking it through each conversation. Miranda had picked up after Danny and Elizabeth had had their turn; she and Kent were settling in until further notice and planning on blowing all the grocery money on pie and ice cream.

"Dad?" Miranda called softly. She came down the stairs in her nightgown and a robe.

Evan, in all his tiredness, blinked until she stopped looking so much like Sherri. "Hey, sweetheart. How's everything?"

"Fine. Danny and Elizabeth were okay when I sent them to bed. They're worried about Matt, though."

Evan kicked off his shoes as he settled into the recliner. "Me too."

"That story in the paper was rude and unnecessary." Miranda came around to sit on the sofa. "Did you tell anyone to shove off?"

Rubbing his forehead with his palm, Evan laughed. "No. Came close, though. Some of the higher-ups don't much care for him."

Miranda frowned. "Is that a problem with your job?"

"Yeah."

They sat quietly for a few moments. Then Miranda shifted on the sofa. "I know I'm the last person in the world you want to hear talk about this, but—if you and Matt are going to be together for, like, the rest of your lives, don't you think your job should be okay with him?"

"I thought they were. I thought he was part of the reason they picked me," Evan said, the words bitter on his tongue. "But it seems like they want a cardboard cutout with a label underneath."

"That's not really you," Miranda laughed. "Like, at all."

"Thank you." Evan slid down in the chair, resting his head back. "So, Miranda, in your opinion as a young adult who is just starting on her career: Should I turn my back on the thing I've done my whole adult life for the person I love? Or do I suck it up and bite the inside of my mouth when they say stupid things to me?"

"Oh!" Miranda appeared to think about the question quite intently. "Well, I guess it depends. Do you love Matt more than your job?"

"I can't really compare the two. Different types of love."

"Like Matt and Mom," she said lightly.

Evan moved his head to look at her. "No. Matt and Mom, that's one side of the spectrum. With you and the rest of the kids. My job is… it's the thing that helped me support my family and accomplish something with my life."

"Oh," Miranda said again. "Then everyone on that side with the family—they don't care what you do for a living."

"True."

"Do you care what you do for a living?"

Evan rolled that around his brain. Yes, he did care. The shield, the uniform, the oath—they meant something. And if that didn't reach the height of how much he loved his family, it did resonate within him.

He wanted to protect people. He wanted to serve.

The only thing he wanted more was for his family to be content and together.

"What do you think Mom would have said?" Evan asked suddenly. "Same advice?"

"I'd like to think she'd say the same thing. But…." Miranda looked away for a moment. "Sometimes I think she sorta hated your job, if I'm honest."

"The hours, the stress," Evan murmured, remembering the fights. The silence.

"You getting crazy focused on your work and forgetting stuff around the house. Made her freaking nuts sometimes." Miranda shivered a little before gathering the blanket on the back of the sofa to lay over her legs. "But she got over it. Got up and went through the next day. Some things are worth putting up with crap for."

"Mom was good like that." Evan struggled for a moment, then sat up. "Thanks, Miranda, for the good advice. I appreciate it."

Miranda smiled brightly. "You're welcome."


EVAN KISSED Miranda good night before going into his own room. He tossed everything into the corner. He just wanted to sleep.

What he did was dream.

# Chapter 29

CAFFEINE FUELED Matt's drive out to the Hamptons. It was late enough to erase the traffic issue, early enough in the season to avoid crowds. He pulled into the driveway at half past eleven, his headlights the only illumination for miles.

"Not creepy or anything," Matt muttered to himself. He pulled out a heavy-duty flashlight and took it with him when he stepped out of the SUV.

In the distance he heard the crashing waves of the ocean, and he smelled the briny scent on the breeze. Swinging the flashlight around, he checked the driveway and the path to the stairs. No footprints or evidence someone had walked here recently.

He walked slowly toward the stairs, swinging the light across the house. The second-floor windows, then the first. The corners of the house.

Nothing out of the ordinary.

At the top of the stairs, Matt paused again. He ran the flashlight everywhere a deep shadow sat, but still, nothing caught his attention.

He used his set of keys to open the front door. From the time he stepped over the threshold until he got to the alarm panel, he had five seconds before 911 would be alerted and the police dispatched.

Front door to panel, Matt took three long strides and keyed in the eight-digit code that identified him as entering.

The quiet darkness of the house settled over Matt. He held his breath and listened, alert for anything that told him he wasn't alone.

Nothing.

Matt continued into the kitchen, then the small room tucked behind the pantry so as to be almost invisible. There, he turned on the only light he would need—the overhead fixture in the room that housed the security equipment.


"HEY, IT'S me."

Jim yawned as he checked his watch. "Everything okay?"

"House is clear. I checked the footage. No one's been out here but the caretaker. There's also a squirrel who seems determined to break in through the kitchen window by any means necessary, but that's it."

"Great. I'm going to get everyone in the car and we'll see you in about two hours." Jim swung his legs over the side of the bed, stretching as he went.

"Coffee'll be ready."

"It better be."


THE PARKING garage provided excellent coverage. Jim watched the entrance as Bennett tucked Griffin, Daisy, and a sleeping Sadie into the backseat. He'd offered to come with them, but Daisy refused. She needed some space, and Bennett needed to get his house in order.

All his pleading eyes and soft apologies were also driving Griffin crazy, and no one wanted him in the same place as Bennett.

"They're ready to go," Bennett said, coming to stand at his side. "I, uh, I could follow in another car."

"No, you couldn't, because then my fiancé would punch you in the face." Jim gave Bennett a cool stare. "And I would probably do the same. Back off, okay? You're never going to get her back if you keep smothering her."

Bennett nodded. Then a sad smile crossed his lips. "I spent a lot of time being paranoid about someone hurting her, and then it turned out to be me who did it."

"That sounds very poetic, but the bottom line is you fucked around. Maybe think about that." Jim didn't wait for an answer—he just really wanted to get the hell out of there.


IN THE limo, Daisy conked out before they even crossed the bridge. Jim played with his phone as Griffin drifted in and out of sleep against his shoulder.

More than anything, he wanted to protect Griffin and, by extension, the people Griffin loved. Bringing Tripp back into their lives like this—he'd had no idea the Pandora's Box he was opening by looking for a way to appease his guilt.

He should have known better.

The FBI was on the case; detectives from numerous cities were combing through their files, looking for links between cold cases and Tripp Ingersoll. Jim had done his job—more than his job. His guilt over the Kellys and not delivering them justice could be assuaged.

But he'd forgotten that Tripp wasn't just an old case, evidence in a report. He was an unstable man who lived in the present, who had had an accomplice all this time, who had a plan he'd been counting on to make him money.

What would he do if cornered?

And the answer to that was… trash Bennett's offices. Which made no sense. Which fit none of his patterns. Unless it was the first step.

The dark sedan outside his house.

Tripp wanted to get to him.

Jim inhaled, exhaled, tightening his hold on Griffin as he felt the gun shift in the holster under his arm.

# Chapter 30

MATT DRANK a bottle of water at the counter of the quiet beach house, lost in thought. He remembered being here for Sadie's christening, when everything felt breezy and light, like the happy vibe would never end.

He flipped through his phone, looking for pictures he'd taken that weekend, wanting to punish himself a little more.

Before he could find anything, the phone vibrated.

"Jim?"

"Yeah, we're on our way."

Matt pushed off from the counter, wandering to the edge of light in the kitchen, then back to look outside through the patio doors. "Everything okay?"

"Seems like it." Short, clipped.

Matt waited for him to spit it out.

"Why are we assuming Tripp's in Toronto?"

"Because he's a serial killer but he understands extradition law?"

Jim's voice was low. "Why did he fly down to talk to Alex himself? Why not send Tracey? Why not hire somebody?"

Matt leaned against the patio doors. Inky black darkness pressed back. "He doesn't have any money."

"Right. Except for what Tracey's friends are slipping her, thinking she's on the run from her crazy husband. That means he's doing the heavy lifting himself."

"He did the break-in."

Jim made a rough sound of frustration. Matt could hear murmuring next to him as he assumed Griffin woke up.

When Jim didn't respond, Matt kicked the wooden panel at the bottom of the door. "He was outside your house."

Still nothing.

"You fucked up his plan."

Matt could hear Jim breathing now, could feel his own heart picking up speed.

He couldn't stand there waiting for something to happen. He went back across the kitchen, heading for the laptop in the surveillance room. "You think they rented a car?" he asked, trying to distract Jim—and to keep himself from going crazy waiting for them to show up. Then he was logging in to some databases he had no business being in.

"He won't use his name."

"She might."

And then something poked Matt in the back of the head. It was Evan, bitching about the bitching from the community board president about the parking situation. Despite the gravity of the situation, Matt started to laugh.

"What?" Jim whispered.

"Parking tickets. The rental company would have had to give her information to the PD if she got a ticket. Give me a few minutes—I'll call you back."

Matt two-finger pecked out Tracey's name in the little white box of the database he wasn't supposed to access. "Come on, sweetheart, where are you?"

A record popped up.

"Two weeks ago in—" *Bingo*. Matt sucked in his breath as he one-handedly redialed Jim's number. He heard a click on the other end and started talking. "Goddammit. She got a parking ticket right in front of Bennett's apartment building." He scrolled down. "Oh shit. A few days ago in Hampton Bay. That's only about a half hour from here."

Jim didn't say anything.

"Jim? Did you hear me? You need to turn around, head back to the city." He heard nothing in response. "Jim?"

When Matt checked the screen, he saw the call had been dropped.


EVAN WOKE with a start. His phone was ringing, Matt's ringtone. He rolled over and grabbed it, swiping across the front to connect the call. "What's wrong?"

"You need to get cars on the LIE—they need to find the limo right now. Jim isn't answering his phone," Matt said, breathless and frantic. "They're here—Tracey and Tripp—out on the Island."

Already out of bed, Evan grabbed clothes out of his closet one-handed. "Are you sure?"

"Parking ticket outside Bennett's apartment, parking ticket in Hampton Bay. Dark sedan rental. They've been watching Jim."

"Shit." Evan pulled on jeans and slipped into his sneakers. "I'm hanging up now. I'll call you back when I get cars on the road."

"I'll be in the car. I'm going to see if I can catch up."

"No—Matt. Just sit tight."

He'd already hung up.


MATT GRABBED his phone and his flashlight as he raced out of the house.


"GRIFFIN, WAKE up," Jim said gently but with urgency. "Griffin, baby. I need you right now."

Griffin came around slowly, blinking and shaking his head. "Are we there?"

"No, but there's a problem." Jim kept his voice low and even. He didn't want Daisy and Sadie to wake up. He didn't want anyone to panic. "I'm not getting any reception on my cell. I need you to check yours." Outside he could make out nothing but trees and empty roadways speeding by.

That seemed to move Griffin into wakefulness a bit quicker. "What's wrong?"

"I don't know, but I need you awake, okay? I need to know you're aware—"

The limo swerved violently. Jim caught Griffin before he could hit the door, and then threw himself across the small space to grab Daisy as she woke in a panic, clutching a screaming Sadie.

"Hold on," Jim shouted, bracing himself against the floor and ceiling, shielding Daisy and the baby as best he could.

They shifted again, a complete turn this time that spun the limo violently. The car collided with something. They heard the crush, felt the crazy vibrations as they spun one more time.

Then the limo came to rest.

# Chapter 31

"EVERYONE OKAY back there?" came the driver's voice over the intercom.

Jim dropped to his knees on the seat and pressed the button. "We're okay," he said, looking at a shaken Griffin and Daisy as they tried to calm Sadie between them. "What happened?"

"Sedan tried to run us off the road. I got us onto the side of the road, though. Wait." The driver paused. "I see cops coming from both ends. Jesus."

"Don't get out of the car," Jim snapped. "Just stay where you are." He scrambled for the door even as Griffin grabbed at him.

"Where are you going?"

"Stay here. No one moves."

Heart beating frantically, Jim pushed the door open. He nearly fell from the limo, adrenaline pumping as he ran toward the road. At least twenty cars had screeched to a halt, all surrounding a dark sedan with heavily tinted windows. He walked toward it, fingers itching like he was a gunfighter at the O.K. Corral as he unbuttoned his jacket to have access to the shoulder holster.

The officers surrounding the sedan had their guns drawn. Someone with a megaphone insisted its occupants exit the vehicle with their hands up.

The passenger door opened a second later. Tracey Baldwin Ingersoll—faithful girlfriend, alibi, and accomplice—came out screaming, hands in the air, crying hysterically as she ran toward the cars.

She babbled to the officers who grabbed her, thanking them in the split second before they pushed her to the ground and handcuffed her.

Jim stood on the edge of the highway where grass met pavement. He couldn't take his eyes off the sedan even as the cops yelled for him to get back.

Then it happened: the driver's door opened and Tripp Ingersoll slid out.

It looked like a peaceful surrender until Tripp looked over and saw Jim.

A sense of serenity fell over Jim in that second. He didn't even reach for his gun. There were cops everywhere, and Jim? Jim was a civilian. A private citizen that Tripp had just tried to run off the road.

"You fucking sonofabitch!" Tripp screamed. He made a move like he was going after Jim, and the moment of distraction allowed the cops to grab him and wrestle him to the ground.

"I'm going to kill you! You think I'm going to stop! I'm going to fucking murder you and your fag boyfriend and that baby! You hear me, you fucking piece of shit? I'm going to cut your throat."

Jim kept smiling. The more he struggled and swung at cops, the more he threatened Jim's life, the deeper he dug his own grave.

Jim waited until they wrestled Tripp into the backseat of the cop car—and then, finally, he turned around and spotted Griffin standing in the tall grass, looking bewildered and lost.

Smile in place, Jim walked over to Griffin and pulled him into his arms.

It was done.


EVAN DROVE with his light flashing on the dashboard, heart in his throat. He listened to the scanner, hearing the entire incident without a visual he so dearly needed. Matt didn't answer his phone, so when Evan braked to a halt at the scene—a chaotic mess of vehicles—he got out and ran into the middle of it.

He found Jim and Griffin first, wrapped in a blanket and leaning against a cop car. Behind them, Evan could see Daisy and Sadie in the backseat.

Phone in hand, he dialed Matt again, hearing each ring like a punch in the stomach.

"Evan? Is everyone all right?"

Blowing out a breath, Evan laughed weakly. "Yeah, everyone's all right."


THE SCENE was chaos until they moved everything off to the side and the traffic was able to pass again. Evan spent thirty minutes on the phone with various officials from the state and the FBI, updating them and pacing up and down the side of the road. Finally, it was done.

They stood on the side of the road for almost thirty minutes, catching each other up, until adrenaline ran out and everyone just wanted to go to bed. There were hugs and tears as they said their good-byes, Jim hovering protectively around Griffin, Daisy, and Sadie, who calmly sucked on a lollipop thanks to a uniform with a sweet tooth.

Evan watched Jim and Matt share a tight hug. Matt whispered, "It's over" and Jim only nodded.

"We'll come out tomorrow at some point, bring you some food," Evan said, lightly pinching Sadie's cheek. "You need anything...."

Another round of hugs and murmured words of concern, and then they were moving in separate directions.


THEY GOT home at sunrise.

Evan and Matt walked through the front door, holding hands as they had been since they drove away from the scene on the expressway. They had been the last to leave, pulling away in Evan's car as Griffin and Jim took off in the opposite direction in Matt's SUV.

"Thank God we're done," Matt sighed as he stripped out of his shoes.

"Done for now. I have to go in in about four hours to explain what happened over the past few days and how it doesn't mean I'm incompetent," Evan said lightly, throwing his suit jacket on the couch as he walked by.

"You just helped catch two serial killers—that's not going to divert this into something positive?" Matt followed him into the kitchen.

"Bad publicity is not why they hired me." Evan pulled open the fridge to stare at the inside. Maybe the answer was sitting there amongst the milk and leftover pasta.

"Fuck 'em."

Evan laughed tiredly as he reached for a bottle of water. "Matt...."

"You did your job. Two murderers are going to jail."

"You and Jim did my job."

Matt made a face as he walked to Evan's side. "You used the resources you had. He's going to jail and so is she. In a few hours, Helena will be in front of the cameras telling everyone two less pieces of shit are walking the streets. And you get to stand there looking...."

"Asleep." Evan shut the door and stepped into Matt's personal space. "I was so fucking scared when you took off."

Matt wrapped his arms around Evan's waist, drawing them together those last few inches. "Pft. I can hold my own. Actually I'm a little sad I got there late. I would have loved to punch that prick in the face."

Evan dropped his head against Matt's shoulder. He still felt faintly sick from that gap of time before he knew where Matt was and what was happening. Losing Matt… the mere thought of it made him breathless with fear. "Stick with security for rich people, please."

Strong hands rubbed down Evan's back. Matt seemed to realize that jokes weren't going to soothe Evan right now. "Okay," he said softly. "I'll take meetings and have to jog off too many lunches and you—you go to the precinct in a few hours and show those assholes that you are the kind of captain they should promote, not hide."

"I don't know if it's worth it."

"Mmm. Okay, no one knows better than me what absolute dickbags they can be," Matt whispered. "But if every good cop walks away for that reason, then they win based on sheer numbers. Don't stay because you want to show them how great a gay captain you can be. Stay and show them what a fucking amazing cop you are."

Evan pressed his face into the curve of Matt's neck. They both needed showers, and more than anything, Evan wanted to say *fuck it* and hand in his resignation. "I haven't been a great cop lately—too much bitching and moaning about paperwork." Evan pulled away so he could look into Matt's eyes. "I think I lost sight of some stuff."

His work.

Matt.

"It's probably because you're old and need glasses," Matt said solemnly before leaning forward and pressing a kiss against Evan's mouth.


THEY SHOWERED together, leaning against the wall because the steamy heat took the last tiny licks of energy from their system. By the time Matt was turning off the bathroom light, he heard doors opening in the hallway—the kids were getting up, getting ready for school.

"You wanna catch them up?" he asked as Evan stumbled past.

"I left a note for Miranda." He beelined for the bed and barely made it under the covers when he got there.

Matt shut off all the lights, then joined him, sinking into the mattress with a noisy exhale. "Let's never do anything like this ever again. My body can't take the strain," he muttered.

"How long before I retire?"

Matt opened his mouth to answer but fell asleep before he could.

WHEN HE woke up, Evan wasn't next to him. The sheets were cool and sunlight streamed through the windows where they'd forgotten to pull the curtains shut.

It was one in the afternoon, according to the clock on the nightstand next to him.

"Shit," Matt muttered. That meant Evan was long gone, and Matt wanted to check on Jim and Griffin.

Downstairs, he found his phone neatly plugged in to the charger by the front door. The house was quiet and neat, and Matt swallowed the urge to hug every piece of furniture. All the chaos of the past few weeks seemed to have been exorcised from their world.

A few texts—Jim told him they were fine and not to bother coming out. He and Griffin were headed home, and Daisy was off to the penthouse. Another from Evan, asking him to come down to the precinct when he woke up.

Matt frowned.

Was he really going to do it? Quit the force? Matt couldn't blame him, but Christ, Evan was supposed to be the Eliot Ness of the NYPD. A straight arrow who rose above the rest of the assholes. Not the guy who said *fuck it* and mic dropped out.

With a heavy heart, Matt went upstairs to get dressed.

# Chapter 32

HELENA, IN a sassy black suit and heels that made her taller than Evan, read through the statement and took press questions with a vaguely superior expression. Evan watched the reporters riveted to her performance as she assured the assembled that Tripp and Tracey were being held until their extradition to Oregon to face first-degree murder charges. She reminded everyone that Captain Cerelli was directly involved in the case, coordinating the efforts to bring the Ingersolls to justice.

"Their reign of unimpeded violence is at an end," she said coolly, then shut the conference down. She gestured for Evan to go first as they stepped off the small stage and then left the room.

In the hallway, after the door slammed closed, Helena did a little touchdown dance. "Oh my God, I'm a natural!"

Evan raised his hand for a high five. "You really are."

She smacked her palm against his. "So does this mean I got the job?"

As he straightened his tie, Evan flashed her a smile. "If I have anything to do with it…."

Helena bounced on her heels. "Fabulous. You need anything else?"

"No, I'm good. You taking off?"

"Shane and I are going over to the penthouse to hang out with Daisy. Then I think we're driving up to see Griffin and Jim."

"Give everyone my love, okay?" He squeezed her arm, already excited to imagine seeing her on a daily basis again. "Hopefully we can head up there over the weekend."

"Shane's out buying a toy store for Sadie." Helena pulled her phone out of her pocket. "Call me if you need anything."

"Thanks again."

Helena gave him a salute. "My pleasure, Captain Cerelli. I'll see you tomorrow."

EVAN FOUND his office occupied by Mr. Higgins and Mr. Alsta. He didn't even blink or acknowledge them until he was sitting at his desk.

"Come to congratulate me?" he asked dryly as the two men exchanged unreadable looks.

"You managed to contain the situation," Mr. Higgins said reluctantly.

"I'm delivering a pair of dangerous serial killers to the Oregon authorities and helping to close several cold-case murders."

Mr. Alsta sighed as he leaned forward, elbows on his knees. "Fine. The press is excellent and just salacious enough for them to keep coming back. That woman—"

"Helena Abbott."

"Decorated police officer and quite adept at dealing with the mess. You want to keep her around?"

Evan couldn't contain the smile entirely as he steepled his fingers under his chin. "She's going to have to be wooed."

Alsta looked at Higgins, who rolled his eyes. "We'll get her a good package."

"Great." Evan regarded them both for a moment. "I guess we're done for now."

Mr. Higgins scowled as he stood. "No more scandals like this, Cerelli. That's not why…." He shut his mouth tightly as he walked to the door.

"Whatever reason you hired me," Evan said slowly, "you ended up with a good cop. And I'm going to show you both how little I need your interference." He grinned widely. "How much you should be afraid if I decide I want your jobs next."

WHEN MATT arrived, the precinct was abuzz and Evan's door was open. A few detectives lingered, and Matt recognized Jesse from GOAL leaning against the doorframe.

"Hey, Matt!" Jesse moved quickly to extend his hand. "Great work."

Matt shrugged, demurely batting his eyelashes. "I have no idea what you're talking about. I'm retired."

Jesse gave him a light punch in the arm. "Of course, my mistake. But I'm taking my detective's exam soon—any pointers you want to give, I'm here to listen."

Matt's ego did a little stretch and preen. "You got my cell number, right? Gimme a call and we'll have a sit-down."

They chatted a bit more before Jesse had to leave for patrol. The rest of the detectives crowded around Evan's desk took their leave one by one, all giving Matt a friendly greeting before the place emptied out.

"You're a folk hero. If you and Jim want free beers, I suggest you start showing up every Friday night," Evan said with a smirk as he leaned back in his chair.

"That sounds like something I can get behind." Matt dropped into the chair across from Evan. "You didn't quit."

"Nope. I got Helena the PR job, though." He looked pleased as punch.

"Nice. Sounds like a full day."

Evan gestured around his office with open arms. "It's not much, but I'm willing to keep it warm for the next captain."

Matt raised his eyebrows. "So not quitting but looking at your next promotion?"

"I got this really amazing pep talk and it made me realize that my job is only worth doing if I believe it is."

"I said that?"

Evan threw a paperclip at him. "If I want to make a difference, I have to take advantage of my position." Evan raised a finger. "No dirty jokes."

Matt did a quick lip zip.

"And that means putting up with the bullshit until I'm in charge and I can make changes."

Matt unzipped. "So are you saying I'm eventually going to be the first lady of New York City?"

"Maybe you start practicing telling people what you're wearing, just in case."

Looking down at his hastily chosen outfit of jeans, a T-shirt, and a sweat jacket, Matt shrugged. "Sears?"

MATT HAD taken the subway to the city, so he and Evan walked to his car shoulder to shoulder. The kids were waiting; dinner had to be eaten.

They had plans for the weekend to check on their friends and plans for the summer when all the family could arrange a week or two to be together.

Evan felt the pieces falling slowly into place: another year, another lesson, another way to make things easier. Maybe they'd never find the perfect solution to everything. Maybe it would never be easy.

"I love you," Evan said when they reached the car.

Matt paused at the passenger's side, his expression pleased. He leaned his arms against the roof of the car. "I love you too."

"You know this is it, right?" Evan matched his position from the driver's side, the rush-hour traffic buzzing behind them. "Us."

"Yesss," Matt said slowly. "I've known that for a while."

The thought had come to Evan quietly and insistently as the day progressed. Some days he believed Matt had brought him back after Sherri died, but really, Matt made him so much better a person.

Better father. Better cop.

A better man.

"I need you to know that. I want to…to… show you how much this is forever…."

Matt's expression went from concerned to amused to a sweet reddening on his cheeks that Evan found to be his favorite reaction, ever.

"The first time you did this—please tell me it was more romantic," Matt murmured.

"Sherri was sitting on the bathroom floor with a pregnancy test in her hand," Evan said ruefully.

Matt started to laugh.

# Chapter 33

*Summer*

DAISY, AN unlimited budget, too much free time on her hands, and free rein brought them to this:

A late-summer wedding in Griffin and Jim's backyard. "Casual" and "simple" translated into floating candles and roses in the pool, long tables under rose arbors on the stretch of property between the house and the garage, and a white runner from the back door to a spot under the big oak tree, where they would take their vows.

Then there were the white balloons and lily garlands and tiny fairy lights woven through anything that didn't move fast enough.

Jim grumbled for all of eight minutes, mostly because when he tried to get some orange juice from the refrigerator, a catering lady kicked him out.

"Someone please bring Jim orange juice so I don't have to drown him in the pool," Daisy said sweetly into her headset. In her lace minidress and crown of tiny roses, she looked like an ethereal angel, though Jim doubted heaven allowed four-inch heels, a push-up bra, and language that made sailors blush.

Jim—not in his tux because of wrinkle concerns—stood like a scolded child on his back steps, waiting for orange juice and someone to save him from the spectacle that was his property.

He stuck his hands in his jeans pockets and contemplated sneaking into the house to find Griffin.

"Don't even think about it!" Daisy drifted by, a clipboard under her arm. Behind her stomped a cheerful Katie in a white halter dress and wellies with little blue whales on them. She was in charge of Sadie, who was also not in her wedding attire for dirt and wrinkling concerns.

"I'm on the same schedule as the toddler," he muttered as the little girl waved.

"Hi, Dim!" No matter how much they tried, the nickname stuck.

Jim enthusiastically waved back, because despite his nerves, he had fatherhood to prepare for.

The sound of a small motorcade arriving pulled Jim off the stairs. He ducked through the trees and bushes lining the side of the house until he came out into the driveway.

The rest of the wedding party had arrived.


MATT STEPPED out of the rented van, blinking in the bright August sun until he slid on his sunglasses. A nice guy named Arthur was their driver, and he had regaled them with stories about the area on the ride over from the hotel.

Matt had best-man duties covered. Right now, it was entertaining Jim out of his funk and putting him in his tux. In about two hours, it would be handing over a ring so Jim and Griffin could do the married thing. After that? He was going to dance the night away with Evan.

While looking fine in a tux.

He whistled a little as he grabbed his bag from the back; Arthur was still telling local history as he handed over Matt's suit bag. Evan joined them a second later, and Matt couldn't resist stealing a kiss.

"What is it with you two?" Miranda asked, suddenly appearing at Matt's elbow. "You're, like, all… kissy."

"Well, Miranda, when two people are in love, they have these urges and…," Matt said slowly, delighting in the face she made at him. "Wait, just ask Kent—I'm sure he can explain it. With his *mouth*."

Kent had started walking toward them, but at Matt's words, he spun and disappeared around the front of the van.

"You are cut off," Evan pointed out, picking up his bag, then following in Kent's footsteps.

"It's two in the afternoon—I haven't had anything to drink yet!"


"THANK GOD" was all Jim said when they walked around the side of the house. The Cerelli girls were dressed in white like Katie, casual and pretty. The guys were in tuxes, something that caused grumbling from everyone with a penis.

Including Jim.

"Black-and-white outdoor wedding—why do the girls get to be more comfortable?" Jim muttered as a passing Drake nephew shoved a carton of orange juice into his hand. Daisy was running Griffin's nieces and nephews like the overseer of Santa's village.

"You want to wear a white dress?" Daisy kept walking by every time he complained. He started to grow concerned that she had him bugged.

Matt put his arm around Jim's shoulders and directed him toward the back door. "Let's get you ready, young man."

JIM WAS in the guest room, fussing with his tie in the mirror. Matt, on the other hand, was doing James Bond moves in the full-length mirror by the closet.

"Seriously? You're supposed to be the adult in charge here," Jim pointed out. He smoothed his hands over his head lest a single tiny hair had decided to move out of formation.

"Well, that was the first mistake made." Matt spun one last time, then did finger guns in Jim's direction. "Hey, you're pretty good-looking. I'd sleep with you."

"Please, say that louder. I want to be thrown out the second-floor window into the pool." Jim checked his cuff links, the crease on his midnight tux. He and Griffin had an agreement that the jacket only had to stay on until they finished pictures and toasts.

"I'm just saying what everyone is thinking," Matt said slowly. He offered his arm, a charming smile on his face. "Ready?"

"Ready."

Jim wanted to be married right the hell now.

MATT STOOD next to Jim under the arch of white roses and lilies. A beaming Richard Drake walked Griffin down the aisle, which pretty much broke every Drake child, spouse, and grandchild into tears. Those who managed to hold it together took one look at Jim's expression and joined in the sniffling.

Reverend Potter, the nice man who had baptized Sadie, had made the drive out to Dutchess County. He said lovely things about Jim and Griffin, about their feelings and journey to this moment. Matt found Evan sitting two rows back, surrounded by the kids, and they shared a little secret smile. Matt winked, then turned his attention to their friends.

"By the power vested in me," Reverend Potter said, and suddenly Matt's own emotions veered out of control. The words coming next meant something, something powerful and particular. Both Jim and Griffin had grown up never imagining this day, let alone a legal marriage license waiting for their signatures, and Matt's and Daisy's.

He felt humbled to be standing there.

JIM AND Matt relaxed in side-by-side deck chairs while everyone under the age of thirty filled the dance floor to do some sort of mass group dance with lots of cha-chaing and butt shaking.

Griffin stood in the midst of a gaggle of sisters, nieces, nephews, the Cerelli children, Mimi—as promised, looking fabulous in a slinky black dress—and Terry Oh. Jim tried not to find it adorable and failed terribly. Taking video from the side were Ben and Liddy, who were narrating the wedding for Nick and Heather back in Seattle. The Heterosexual Power Cabal had gotten their wish today.

Jim was a happily married man.

"Your face is so gross," Matt deadpanned.

"Shut up." Jim raised his bottle of beer and clinked it against Matt's.

"Your husband is ridiculously cute, you know that, right?"

"No, I missed that. I'm just in it for the sex." Jim sighed before taking a sip of his beer. "And tax benefits."

A very pregnant Farrah Drake waved from across the way, tottering across the lawn; she was on her third piece of cake, claiming Jim's offspring had a sweet tooth. Only the fear of Farrah's temper kept Jim in his chair and not offering his arm so she could navigate the plush lawn and patio brick. Apparently he had a tendency to hover over their surrogate/his sister-in-law, who was currently incubating their baby, and this annoyed her.

He'd been reprimanded more than once.

"So that must be weird," Matt whispered, hiding behind his bottle, probably in case Farrah read lips.

"Having my sperm inside my husband's sister? No, it's entirely normal and doesn't freak me out at all."

Matt whistled lightly. "I'm glad I got my kids when they were potty trained."

"Now you're just bragging."

Jim leaned his head back and watched the dance floor. The group dance was over, but Griffin still bounced among the teens to toddlers swirling around him. His hair product had lost its battle with the humidity hours ago, and Griffin had acquiesced to Jim's request that he wear his glasses.

"Kinky bastard," Griffin had said, delighted.

"Your lovesick face makes me feel things," Matt sighed.

"I was actually making your face when you look at your boyfriend. Did I get it right? Did you feel a slight twinge of nausea as if you've smelled sewage?"

Matt let out a cackle, attracting the attention of everyone currently not attempting to do the Time Warp on the dance floor.

"So when are you taking the plunge?" Jim asked, curious because while he could think of no two people more "married" than Evan and Matt, he wondered when he'd be whipping the tux out for their nuptials.

But Matt shrugged. "Eh. This isn't our scene—not that it isn't wonderful, and I love wearing these tight shoes, but I feel like our plunger plunged a long time ago."

Jim took another sip of beer. "Not even a courthouse wedding?"

"Too flashy."

"Flashy? Good Lord. I tried for that and Griffin death glared me."

"Like I said," Matt said softly. "Not our scene.

Jim followed his gaze to where it rested—of course—on Evan, who was dancing with his youngest daughter on the edge of the dance floor. There was a look of lightness and joy on his face as he gave her a twirl, and Jim could barely find the tense, terse man he had met those years ago.

And no darkness in his friend Matt—none at all.

"Well, whatever your scene is, I hope you guys will be on hand for parenting questions as they come up."

"You have Evan's cell number. Once you get your little one up to year eight, give me a holler."

"Maaatt! Come dance with me," Katie shrieked as she ran by, clearly the victim of free-flowing champagne and being over twenty-one.

"Oh Jesus." Matt scrambled out of the chair, catching Katie before she could end up in the pool. Jim watched them tango onto the dance floor, and then an impromptu dance competition between the dads and their daughters broke out. Things got interesting when Griffin's fleet of brothers-in-law joined in with their girls. Then Griffin grabbed Richard away from his girlfriend's side and Jim thought his face might split in two from the smile that bloomed.

In a few years that would be Jim and Griffin with their little girl, and the thought made Jim the happiest man there—despite stiff competition.

"HOW LONG before the baby's here?" Evan asked as he and Griffin waited for the bartender to return with more bottled water. They were both jacketless and sweating, more from dancing as the sun had finally set.

"Five weeks." Griffin laughed before making a strangled face. "I'm so freaked out. Like excited, but holy crap."

"That sounds about right," Evan said dryly. "Skipping the honeymoon—you sure that's a good idea? Chances are you won't get this chance again for a while."

"Eh, we did Hawaii for a year and probably hit every beautiful beach while we were traveling. Now we just want to stay home and enjoy our lives." Every time someone asked them the same question, Griffin felt utter peace with his answer.

They'd both been running for such a long time. This was their time to stop and be.

"Plus, we have a built-in babysitter," Griffin added.

Daisy had bought the house next door—literally—and she and Sadie were already moved in. Bennett was still around, dutifully attempting to rebuild things with his wife. He lived in the city but had recently purchased a smaller house a few miles away, his way of proving he was serious about getting back together.

"I was surprised to see him here, actually."

Griffin made a face. "Yeah. I had this whole speech about no way José plotted out, but Jim said Daisy's sad face outweighed my logic." He stole a tiny pink umbrella from the bartender's prep area. "I think that's an insult."

"You think she's going to take him back?"

"She already has. She just hasn't told him that."

Evan chuckled. "Let him suffer a bit more?"

"God, yes. I'm glad, though—it proves she still has a spine."

The bartender returned with a case of water, then gave each of them two. They had thirsty dance partners to share with.

"So Daisy and Bennett are patching it up, me and Jim are old married dudes, Shane and Helena are still in the ass-grabbing honeymoon phase, which—bless. What about you?"

Evan squinted at Griffin. They dodged the tables and various clumps of chairs where people had created their own little huddles. "What about me?"

"Oh come on, Evan. When are you guys making it permanent?"

"About three years ago." Evan laughed at the face Griffin made. "What?"

"You're never going to do it?"

"What? Ass-grab in public? Probably not."

Griffin put the wet bottle to his forehead, pretending to swoon. "Did you just say ass?"

"Yes. That's your wedding present."

At the edge of the dance floor, they waited; the kids were all dancing, flailing their arms and spinning as the DJ flashed lights and set bubbles loose. There was barely any open space—the dancing even spilled out onto the grass for those who felt more secure out of arm's reach of the younger set.

"Thank you," Evan said suddenly, catching Griffin's attention.

"For what?"

"When I met you, I was struggling with a lot of things. You were very kind to me when you didn't have to be, and I... I appreciate it."

Griffin made another face—one where he was trying not to get sappy emotional, because he was sure he was over the quota for today. "That's a very touching thing to say when we were actually talking about sex," he said, his sniffles ruining the playful tone.

"Sex is important to a relationship," Evan deadpanned. "If you need any advice in that department...."

Griffin leaned his head on Evan's shoulder, feeling stupidly sentimental even as he laughed. "You're a good guy, Evan Cerelli, and I'm glad you're my friend."

# Epilogue

THEY LEFT their tux jackets on the kitchen counter amongst the empty champagne bottles and remnants of the caterer's prep for the buffet. Griffin kicked off his shoes in the hallway, pulling Jim toward the last door on the right.

This was the only room people weren't allowed in.

This was a secret until Farrah delivered and Jim and Griffin could bring their daughter in here for the first time.

"Isn't it a little weird to drink champagne in a nursery?" Jim asked as Griffin opened the door.

"Only if you're sharing with the baby."

A tiny lamp in the shape of a ceramic bunny was all the light Griffin allowed. He opened the sheer white curtains across the trio of windows so the lights from the wedding reception below cast patterns across the polished wood floors and dark red area rug. He knew the entire room by heart—the cherry-blossom wallpaper, the blond wood crib and matching dresser and changing table. The pale pink linens and assortment of bunnies on every surface.

Everything was ready and waiting for Caroline Kelly Shea-Drake (or Drake-Shea—they were still negotiating).

Griffin's face ached with the smiling he'd been doing all day—all week, really. The utter joy that was marrying Jim left him giddy and stupid and breathlessly happy. And right now? Imagining their baby here took the rest of his breath away.

He turned around to find Jim sitting on the floor, leaning against the tall dresser, sprawled and gorgeous, with a bottle of ridiculously expensive champagne in his hand. Griffin's heart stuttered.

"What?" Jim asked. Tie askew and bathed in shadows, he looked like a supermodel trying to entice you to buy... anything. Let's face it, Griffin would buy anything Jim was selling, for the rest of their lives.

"Nothing. You're just so handsome, and now you're all mine," Griffin said lightly before dropping to the floor and crawling toward Jim.

Jim laughed, low and dirty. "Oh my goodness, that's quite interesting, Mr. Drake."

Griffin shrugged as he straddled Jim's lap. "Mr. Drake-Shea."

"Shea-Drake."

"We're going to need to make a final decision on this at some point," Griffin said, reaching for the bottle of champagne. "I vote that point is not now."

"I'm not having sex with you in our daughter's nursery." Jim declared it in his full authority voice, and Griffin squirmed in his arms.

"Agreed, so stop using that voice."

"We can make out a little, though," he teased, rubbing his hands down Griffin's back.

They kissed slowly, enjoying the build. Griffin closed his eyes, sucking Jim's bottom lip as he fought to keep his hips still. Because they weren't going to have sex in their daughter's room.

Jim pulled back, his smile so delightful and pleased that Griffin kissed his nose.

"I love you, and I'm glad I married you," Griffin murmured, wrapping his arms around Jim's neck, resting against his shoulders. "And I'm also glad you and my sister are having our baby, which doesn't sound weird at all."

They shared a laugh.

Through the windows came the sounds of music and conversation, their families and friends mixing together.

"We have to say thank you and good night." Sighing, Griffin curled up in Jim's arms, thinking about how many apology calls he'd have to make if he just didn't move.

"Yeah, we should do that," Jim said, reaching for the champagne beside them. "Right after we drink this bottle."

There was so much to celebrate—the wedding, the baby, their lives being settled in a way it had never been before. They were anchored now, with a home and a future they'd decided on. Everyone had been drinking the caterers dry for the past three hours, but this felt like something else.

Griffin shifted just enough so Jim could pop the cork with both hands.

"We don't have glasses," Griffin pointed out as the cork came free and Jim conveniently used his mouth to suck up the stream coming out. "Ah, never mind," he added as Jim did rude things to the opening of the bottle.

"First toast," Jim said, licking his lips. "To cheeky young men who strong-arm dates from cranky old cops."

"That cupcake thing was pretty awesome." Griffin preened as he took the bottle and drank.

"You sang me happy birthday," Jim murmured. Even after all this time, the look on Jim's face when he remembered that first night was pure bliss to Griffin.

"I never wanted to leave."

"Technically you didn't...."

They laughed and passed the bottle a few more times.

"Second toast," Griffin said, taking control of what was left of the champagne. "To my hero, James Shea. The best person I've ever met in my life. Gorgeous and sexy and smart and amazingly brave. You make me a better human being, and I hope our Caroline turns out exactly like you in every respect. Except for the hair."

Jim ran a defensive hand over his shorn hair, still holding on to its color; Griffin suspected gray was actually too frightened of Jim to grow in. "What's wrong with my hair?"

"Baby with a buzz cut just doesn't do it for me." Griffin leaned down, grinding his hips slowly.

"Mmmm." Jim took the bottle away—Griffin heard it clink against the floor—and returned both arms around Griffin's middle. "Caroline should have your gorgeous hair," Jim murmured, rubbing his warm hands against the length of Griffin's back.

"Don't talk sexy to me and say her name," Griffin whispered, slotting his hips just enough to catch their straining erections against each other. "So stop saying her name and keep talking sexy."


JIM OPENED his mouth, trailed his hands down to squeeze Griffin's spectacularly tuxedoed ass. His husband (that would take some getting used to) flicked their tongues together and then gave him a lap dance that Jim was sure sparked out his brain.

Let those people keep laughing and dancing down there. The DJ was paid until ten, the champagne stock holding on....

He just wanted to stay here with the love of his life in his arms, in this room that symbolized everything about the beautiful future ahead.

Everything else could wait.

"I CAN'T believe no one has figured this out," Evan murmured into Matt's ear as they twirled around the dance floor.

Matt tightened his arms around Evan's waist, slotting them close together in a way that bordered on dirty.

Evan didn't care.

"Especially since they're such nosy sons of bitches."

They moved slowly, trading off who was leading like it was second nature. They were getting good at this, the give and take, letting instinct be their guide instead of thinking too hard.

Evan knew, in the quiet of the moment, that this was their real secret. How they made this work—made them work.

Trust.

Letting go.

"Stop thinking so loud. This is romantic," Matt whispered, ending his words with a kiss against the curve of Evan's ear.

It *was* romantic, cradled in Matt's arms, the whirling dervish of the night settling around them.

"We could make an announcement," he said, thinking of the kids' excitement, Jim and Griffin's support, Helena and Shane's enthusiasm.

"Or we could keep it a secret like we agreed." Matt moved his head just enough to give Evan a look.

"Fine." Evan laid his head back on Matt's shoulder. A secret just for them. Yes, that seemed right.

The DJ switched songs but not tempos: an old Motown song that invited more couples to the dance floor. Evan saw love in every stage—blushing teens to folks just grateful to have an intimate moment away from the kids to the smooth dancing moves of those who'd been doing this for decades.

This wasn't the way his life was supposed to go, but this was exactly where he decided to be.

Don't miss

Faith, Love, & Devotion:
Book One

*Faith &
Fidelity*

By Tere Michaels

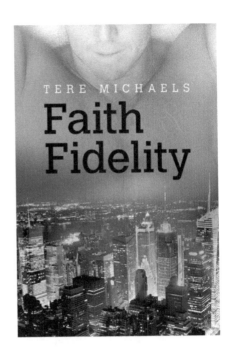

Reeling from the recent death of his wife, police officer Evan Cerelli looks at his four children and can only see how he fails them. His loving wife was the caretaker and nurturer, and now the single father feels himself being crushed by the pain of loss and the heavy responsibility of raising his kids.

At the urging of his partner, Evan celebrates a coworker's retirement and meets disgraced former cop turned security consultant Matt Haight. A friendship born out of loneliness and the solace of the bottle turns out to be exactly what they both need.

The past year has been a slow death for Matt Haight. Ostracized from his beloved police force, facing middle age and perpetual loneliness, Matt sees only a black hole where his future should be. When he discovers another lost soul in Evan, some of the pieces he thought he lost start to fall back in place. Their friendship turns into something deeper, but love is the last thing either man expected, and both of them struggle to reconcile their new and overwhelming feelings for one another.

http://www.dreamspinnerpress.com

Faith, Love, & Devotion:
Book Two

*Love &
Loyalty*

By Tere Michaels

Seattle Homicide Detective Jim Shea never takes work home with him—until now. A judge banged his gavel, declared a defendant not guilty, and laid waste to a family. The emotional fallout of the trial leaves Jim vulnerable and duty-bound to the victim's dying father.

It's that man's story that screenwriter Griffin Drake and his best friend, actress Daisy Baylor, see as their ticket out of action blockbusters and into more serious fare. But to get the juicy details, Griffin needs to win over the stoic and protective Detective Shea. Their attraction is immediate, and Daisy encourages Griffin to use it to their advantage: secure the man, secure the story. Neither man has had much luck when it comes to love, and when their one night together evolves into a long weekend of rapidly intensifying feelings, both Griffin's fierce loyalty to Daisy and his very career is put to the test.

Because the more Griffin is drawn into a new life with Jim, the more his Hollywood life falls apart. Secrets and broken trust threaten Griffin's relationships, and he'll have to choose between telling the truth or writing a Hollywood ending.

http://www.dreamspinnerpress.com

Faith, Love, & Devotion:
Book Three

*Duty &
Devotion*

By Tere Michaels

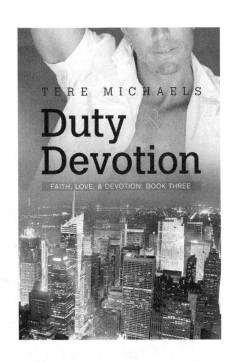

A year after deciding to share their lives, Matt and Evan are working on their happily ever after—which isn't as easy as it looks. As life settles down into a routine, Matt finds happiness in his role as the ideal househusband of Queens, New York, but he worries about Evan's continued workaholic—and emotionally avoidant—ways. Trying to juggle his evolving relationship with Evan and his children, Matt turns to his friend, former Seattle Homicide Detective Jim Shea.

The continued friendship between Matt and Jim is a thorn in Evan's side. Jealous and uncomfortable with imagining their brief affair, Evan struggles to come to terms with what being in a committed relationship with a man means, and the implications about his love for his deceased wife, the impact on his children, and how other people will view him. His turmoil threatens his relationship with Matt, who worries that Evan will once again chose a life without him. But now, the stakes are much higher.

http://www.dreamspinnerpress.com

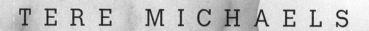

# TERE MICHAELS

# Cherish &
# Blessed

FAITH, LOVE, & DEVOTION: BOOKS FOUR & FIVE

## Cherish

After several years of happy coupledom, Matt and Evan can relax in the knowledge that their little family has survived the worst of it. The two older girls are away at college, the twins have yet to fully hit teen angst, Matt is doing well with his part time security consulting, and Evan is about to be promoted to captain—it seems like things are calm and bright.

Until they aren't.

As the holidays approach, Evan and Matt get a shock no parent is ever prepared for: feisty Miranda, Evan's eldest, has a new boyfriend, Kent, and they are talking marriage after just three months together. In fact, Miranda wants to bring him to Thanksgiving dinner—along with his parents, Blake and Cornelia.

## Blessed

Lives are in transition as everyone gathers at the stunning Hamptons beach home of Daisy and Bennett to celebrate the christening of their new baby. Griffin and Jim—secretly growing tired of their rootless lifestyle—are in a rocky spot in their relationship. And as the godfather, Griffin finds himself yearning for something he's sure Jim won't be interested in.

Fatherhood.

Matt and Evan are looking to reconnect during the long weekend, as their respective careers pull them in separate directions. With less time spent together, Evan grows concerned about what will happen when the last two kids leave the nest.

# http://www.dreamspinnerpress.com

TERE MICHAELS unofficially began her writing career at the age of four when she learned that people got paid to write stories. It seemed the most perfect and logical job in the world and after that, her path was never in question.

(The romance writer part was written in the stars—she was born on Valentine's Day.)

It took thirty-six years of "research" and "life experience" and well… life… before her first book was published, but there are no regrets (she doesn't believe in them). Along the way, she had some interesting jobs in television, animation, arts education, PR, and a national magazine—but she never stopped believing she would eventually earn her living writing stories about love.

She is a member of RWA, Rainbow Romance Writers, and Liberty States Fiction Writers. Her home base is a small town in New Jersey, very near NYC, a city she dearly loves. She shares her life with her husband, her teenaged son—who will just not stop growing—and three exceedingly spoiled cats. Her spare time is spent watching way too much sports programming, going to the movies and for long walks/runs in the park, reading her book club's current selection, and volunteering.

Nothing makes her happier than knowing she made a reader laugh or smile or cry. It's the purpose of sharing her work with people. She loves hearing from fans and fellow writers, and is always available for speaking engagements, visits and workshops.

Find her at:
Website: http://www.teremichaels.com
Facebook: https://www.facebook.com/tere.michaels
Twitter: @TereMichaels

# One Night Ever After

By Tere Michaels, Elle Brownlee, and Elizah J. Davis

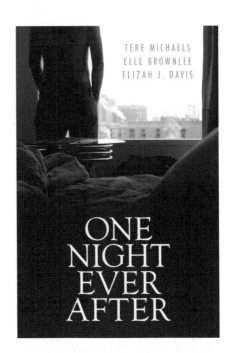

## Just a Drive
by Tere Michaels

After weeks of flirting, "One Night" Wyatt Walsh spends a fabulous night with his shy coworker, Benji Trammell. As Wyatt tries to sneak out the next morning, he receives a call from his frantic, very pregnant best friend Raven—she needs him immediately. With no other way to get from New York City to the Pennsylvania town where Raven and her husband live, Wyatt accepts Benji's offer to drive him there. Wary and unsure of each other, they start the trip at odds, but as time goes on, the barriers that usually keep people at a distance fail. And what started out as "just a drive" becomes a step toward romance.

# http://www.dreamspinnerpress.com

# One Holiday Ever After

By Tere Michaels, Elle Brownlee, and
Elizah J. Davis

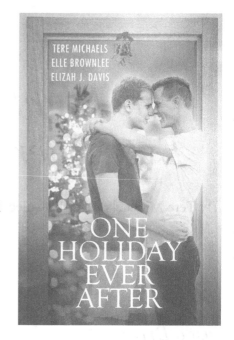

## Holiday Roommates
by Tere Michaels

As an actor without prospects, Nate Brandywine needs an emergency roommate for the month of December. During a humiliating gig as a Christmas elf at a NYC department store, he meets Sean Callahan, his producer and a man struggling under the weight of a past-due loan. Sean's desperate for a place to stay in the city for a few weeks. A month of sharing a workplace and an apartment with someone you can't stop flirting with? Maybe the holidays won't be so terrible after all.

# http://www.dreamspinnerpress.com

# Who Knows the Storm

By Tere Michaels

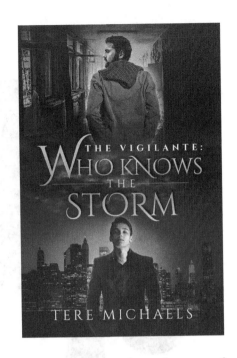

In a dystopian near future, New York City has become the epicenter of decadence—gambling, the flesh trade, a playground for the wealthy. And underneath? Crime, fueled by "Dead Bolt," a destructive designer drug. This New City is where Nox Boyet leads a double life. At night, he is the Vigilante, struggling to keep the streets safe for citizens abandoned by the corrupt government and police. During the day, he works in construction and does his best to raise his adopted teenaged son, Sam.

A mysterious letter addressed to Sam brings Nox in direct contact with "model" Cade Creel, a high-end prostitute working at the Iron Butterfly Casino. Suspicion gives way to an intense attraction as dark figures from Nox's past and the mysterious peddlers of Dead Bolt begin to descend— and put all their lives in danger. When things spin out of control, Cade is the only person Nox can trust to help him save Sam.

## http://www.dreamspinnerpress.com

CPSIA information can be obtained at www.ICGtesting.com
Printed in the USA
LVOW01s0608160415

434745LV00012B/92/P

9 781632 167101